CYBER'S UNDERGROUND

Sapiens Run Book 3

JAMIE DAVIS

MedicCast Productions

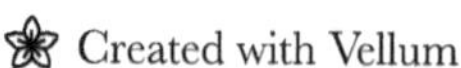 Created with Vellum

Also by Jamie Davis

Sapiens Run Trilogy

Book 1 - *Cyber's Change*

Book 2 - *Cyber's Escape*

Book 3 - *Cyber's Underground*

—

The Delivery Mage (5 Urban Fantasy books)

Book 1 - *Deliver or Die*

—

The Broken Throne Series (5 Urban Fantasy books)

Read book 1 - *The Charm Runner*

—

The Accidental Traveler LitRPG Trilogy

(with C.J. Davis)

Read book 1 - *The Accidental Thief*

—

Accidental Champion LitRPG Trilogy 2

(with C.J. Davis)

Read book 1 - *Accidental Duelist*

—

Extreme Medical Services Series (8 Urban Fantasy books)

Read book 1 - Extreme Medical Services

—

Eldara Sister Series (2 Historical Fantasy books)

Read book 1 - *The Nightingale's Angel*

—

Follow on Facebook for updates, news, and upcoming book excerpts

Facebook.com/jamiedavisbooks

—

To my LGBTQ+ family, friends, and friends I've yet to meet. Stand tall, for this papa-bear and many other allies stand with you.

Chapter 1

"HOW DID they find us again so quickly?" Cass asked as she shoved her clothes in her backpack. She clipped it closed and shrugged her shoulders into the straps.

Shelby shook her head. "I don't know. We don't have time to worry about that. Ramona said to leave the motel and meet her up on the highway ramp leading to the interstate."

"We're in the middle of nowhere, Shelby. I can't believe anyone knows who we are or that we're hiding out here."

"You heard Ramona's message. She thinks they're tracking your implant somehow. We figured as much the last time they almost caught us. She must have found some confirming evidence while she was out searching for the gear we'll need to mask it from prying eyes. We just have to give her time to figure it out."

Cass followed Shelby out the motel room door into the darkness. The small roadside inn only had twenty-five rooms situated in a low, single-story structure. It sat beside a twenty-four-hour diner and an automobile charging station, just off the Pennsylvania Turnpike.

Shelby stooped in the shadows by the door, looking for any hints of a threat. Across the dark gravel parking lot, the flickering neon sign of the Shady Rest Motel provided an orange-red glow that barely lit up the night. The standard overhead parking lot lights were either broken or turned off.

Cass dialed in the night-vision capability in her ocular implant and scanned the area.

Shelby glanced her way as she waited by the door. "See anything, Cass?"

Cass shook her head, scanning the parking lot that now looked as bright as day, thanks to her enhanced vision. "No, it's clear. Let's get across the road first. There are some bushes and trees over there. We can walk that way to the highway ramp."

Shelby nodded and let Cass lead the way in the dark. Cass continued to scan the area as she jogged toward the road. She didn't see anyone. Though her auditory implant picked up the hum of the occasional car or transport on the highway, there were no cars out this time of night here near the rest stop.

The whole place was deserted, but that was no surprise. Cass didn't expect to see anyone out and about this late in the small, central Pennsylvania town. It was one of the reasons Ramona had picked this particular motel. Isolation would make any strangers stand out among the locals.

They picked up speed as they crossed the open space around the roadway, heading toward the trees on the other side.

As they reached the trees and stopped to catch their breath, Cass glanced back at Shelby and whispered, "Did Ramona say anything about whether she was able to find the equipment she needed from her contact out here?"

"You got the same message from her I did." Shelby crouched by one of the trees and turned to look back the way they'd come.

"There's no one following us, Shelby." Cass tapped the side of her head next to her right eye. "I can see in the dark way better than you can. Come on. We should keep moving. I want to get to the rendezvous and see what Ramona was able to pick up."

Shelby smiled and reached out for Cass's hand as they walked through the brush and trees along the road's edge. "I'm sure she's found something that'll help. She was able to reboot my implant with a new locator identity."

"Except that she's had trouble doing the same for my implant. What's wrong with me?"

Cass thought back to the four times Ramona had tried to reset her implant's firmware and identifier code so far. It had been a week since Shelby and her cousin had helped Cass escape the Sapiens Movement enclave where her family lived.

Each time Ramona made the attempt, she had assured Cass she'd be able to reset the cerebral cybernetic implant in a way that would make her untraceable via the Mantle. The worldwide AI network, known as the Mantle, linked all connected devices in the modern world, including those individuals with cybernetic implants.

After the fourth failed attempt, Ramona had left them at this motel while she went to a nearby cybernetics wholesale depot. She claimed to have an old friend who worked at the warehouse who could help her put together whatever workaround she had in mind. Given Ramona's limited track record so far, Cass wasn't as sure of the hacker's abilities as Shelby was.

That last attempt at a reset, something Ramona had called a crash restore had left Cass with a splitting headache that had lasted for hours after they'd disconnected the hard-wired interface.

Shelby stopped and smiled at Cass in the darkness. "Cassie, look, my cousin is good at what she does. You heard her when she dropped us off this morning. There's something strange about what's going on with your implant and she's got to figure it out first. Remember, your cerebral implant is much more extensive than mine. It's not only connecting you to the Mantle and other things in the world; it also has essential systems that saved your life after the accident. Don't forget that."

"I won't forget it, Shel. I'll never forget it. That's how we ended up in this mess to begin with. Now, my father and Simon Cantwell have chased me halfway across the state to try and bring me back. They won't stop hounding us until they retrieve the video files from my implant."

Shelby gave Cass's fingers a gentle squeeze and then tugged a little as they both turned and headed off again, paralleling the road as they headed toward the ramp leading up to the interstate.

They didn't have to hide and wait for very long. About five minutes after they got to the cluster of bushes growing near the road, a white van with tinted windows pulled up in the darkness. The passenger window rolled down and Ramona's voice came from inside, "Come on. Hurry up and jump in. We need to get out of here. They can't be too far away, based on the message I intercepted."

Cass and Shelby darted from their hiding place and jumped into the small delivery van. It was the same one they'd used to rescue Cass from the enclave.

As they climbed in and Cass shut the door, Ramona stomped on the accelerator and the electric vehicle sped off up the ramp and back onto the highway. It looked like they were heading west again. Ramona thought maybe they'd head to Pittsburgh tonight and find a place to hide out while working on Cass's implant.

Cass shrugged out of her backpack, laying it behind the seat. Something Ramona said as they'd run to the van came back to her.

"What kind of message did you intercept, Ramona? I would have thought they'd be using secure communications instead of something you could listen in on."

"The message was in the code of the bot they used to track you down over the Mantle. It had a creation and location timestamp in it. They were only about twenty miles to the east when the bot homed in on you."

Cass turned and stared out the back window the way they came, searching for any signs of pursuit. It scared her to know they were so close this time.

Seeing no headlights behind them, she looked behind the rear seat of the van to the cargo area and spotted several open cardboard boxes full of various pieces of electronic equipment and wire harnesses. It seemed to be the same random collection of gear Ramona already had when they'd rescued Cass.

Cass turned back to the front. "Did you get what you were looking for?"

"Yeah, I'm pretty sure I found the circuit board I need to create a firmware scanner I want to use on your implant. When we get to the next rest stop, we'll pull off into one of the overnight rest areas and see what we can do."

Ramona's clipped words and tone reminded Cass just how frustrated the hacker was with the difficulty in cracking the problem with Cass's implant. Ramona had initially said it would be a quick fix. That had been six days ago. Yesterday, she remarked that it had become one of the most challenging hacks of her career.

Cass didn't like the sound of that. She hoped it didn't turn out to be impossible. She shuddered as she remembered what her father and Simon had planned for her back in the enclave. If they caught up to the trio— Well, Cass didn't want to think about it. She'd rather die than fall into Simon Cantwell's hands again.

The girls drove for more than an hour before reaching a rest area with picnic tables and a public restroom. Shelby jumped out and headed for the bathroom while Cass stood beside the van and stretched her hands over her head.

Behind her, Ramona had climbed into the back of the van. She fidgeted with a portable computer rig she'd cobbled together from a variety of systems and devices. It all attached to Ramona's implant with a crude wire harness running up her arm. Rubber bands clamped the harness at various places along her arm until it reached the side of her head. The whole thing jacked into a port in the cerebral implant that circled the back of Ramona's head like a broad silver horseshoe.

"Cass, while we wait for Shelby to come out, open up a narrowband, local connection to me. I want to renew the masking protocol I had in place before their bot found you."

Cass sighed and mentally activated the internal wireless port in her implant's firewall. She had done this so many times, her system automatically connected to Ramona as soon as the port opened.

"What's going to keep them from breaking through this one like the last time?"

"Look, Cass, I'm sorry that it's taking me so long to do this. I'm really good at what I do. Believe me when I tell you no one else could do more than I've been doing to reset your system to a new, clean serial number. This should be a piece of cake. There's something strange going on with your implant and I can't figure out what it is."

"You were able to redo Shelby's in just a couple of hours. She told me."

"Yeah, and I should've been able to do the same for you, too. The first two times should've worked but your system has some sort of patch on it that I can't get around."

"Does it have to do with what Derek did, when he installed his *Protocol One* hacking program in my implant, so that I could get into the enclave undetected? I haven't been able to open that file since the last time I tried to breach the firewall there. It's corrupted beyond repair according to my system diagnostic."

Ramona shook her head and met Cass's eyes. "I thought at first that might be it. Derek and his hacks are legendary. I've never met him, but he's supposed to be among the very best. I tried to open the *Protocol One* file in your system the last time I tried to wipe the firmware. It's fully corrupted, almost like the code inside melted into a mass of random ones and zeros. Your system seems to have walled it off so it isn't accessing your implant anymore. If there's something it's still connected to that's hampering the reset, I can't find it."

"Can't you reach out to Derek and see if he can help?"

"I've tried. He's a hard guy to get ahold of under normal circumstances. Now though, it's like he's disappeared entirely. I've got inquiries out to try and leave messages for him in various places I trust but I'm not sure he'll get the messages. If he's gone fully underground for some reason, he won't surface for a while."

A chime sounded in Cass's mind as Ramona's system completed the connection with hers.

"I've joined to your implant wirelessly, Cass. Why don't you go ahead and use the bathroom. I can get started from here with the initial stages of this diagnostic sweep. I'll get the rest of my gear set up here, in the back of the van, while you're gone. Once you're back, Shelby can keep watch while I try to dial into your system again and we'll see if we can't run that override I came up with. First, though, let's try to see what's going on before we get started again."

Cass nodded and headed off toward the small brick building in the center of the rest area. It was just old enough to still have separate men's and women's restrooms. Shelby emerged as Cass walked up the sidewalk from the parking lot.

Shelby threw an arm across her shoulder, pulling her close for a kiss.

Cass savored it along with her girlfriend's embrace. She nodded to the women's room. "What's it like in there?"

"It's not the worst bathroom I've ever been in." Shelby laughed. "I guess we just have to take what we can find."

Cass smiled, kissed Shelby again and then went inside.

Shelby was right, sort of. It wasn't that the facilities weren't clean. The bathroom was old and everything looked more than a little beat up and in desperate need of replacement.

Cass went ahead and did what she came to do, then stopped at the sink to wash her hands. She splashed some water on her face and stood staring at herself in the mirror.

Cass noted the sunken eyes with dark circles under them. She hadn't put on any makeup in days, or had a real chance to relax and clean up. She was a mess.

She dried her hands with the automated blower on the wall and headed back toward the van.

Shelby was leaning up against the passenger side of the vehicle, sipping soda from a can. She hooked a thumb over her shoulder toward the back seat. "Go ahead inside. Ramona's got everything all set up for you. I'll stay out here to keep an eye out."

Cass nodded and climbed in the back. Ramona had spun the front passenger seat around to face the rear. She sat there with a large laptop computer propped next to her atop a cardboard box. Beside it, a cable led to a tablet screen on a plastic stand sitting on the rear bench seat.

Having been through this before, Cass lay down on the long back seat so that her head rested on the armrest closest to the door.

Ramona moved the tablet on the stand. Now it sat next to Cass's head.

Cass looked up at Ramona as the other girl leaned over her. "This isn't going to hurt like the last time, is it?"

"Honestly, honey, it shouldn't have hurt any of the times. I don't know what caused that. Something that Sapiens IT guy did back at the enclave caused a feedback loop. When he used the security fire-wall to crash your implant's systems, he created sub-routines I've never seen before. I tripped the loop by accident the first time I tried to overwrite your implant's firmware. Since then, I've been able to partially bypass it for the most part, but not completely. I'm sorry it's hurting you."

"I don't understand why you can't remove it, or the file Derek installed."

Ramona placed a reassuring hand on Cass's shoulder. "I'm still not sure what exactly it was he did. For a guy who supposedly hates modern technologies, he's sure created some unique uses for it."

Cass didn't like the way Ramona seemed more and more unsure of herself each time they tried this. She knew the older girl wasn't trying to hurt her.

Cass nodded and said, "I just want to know what to expect. That's all."

"Hopefully, I'll plug-in and you'll fall asleep for a little bit. Then, when you wake up, everything will be normal, and no one will be able to track you anymore."

Cass hoped it was that easy, but the previous four failures had not instilled much hope in her that it would work this time.

Ramona reached out and pressed on the silver metal of Cass's implant, right next to her ear. She moved aside a hidden panel and approached with a pair of fine wires. Each one ended in a small, round plug, kind of like what you would have used with an old pair of wired earbuds.

Cass felt a little pressure as Ramona held her head still and snapped both plugs into place.

Ramona smiled down at her. "Okay, close your eyes. Next time you wake up, we'll have things all figured out."

Cass smiled back, closed her eyes, and everything went black.

Chapter 2

SIMON CANTWELL CLIMBED out of the black SUV and walked across the gravel parking lot to the open door of the motel room. Three of his men poked around inside the room, searching for any trace of the girl. When he stepped inside, one of them stood up and turned to face him at attention.

"We must've just missed them, sir. They can't have been gone that long, and it looks like they had to leave in a hurry. They left food and a few of their belongings behind this time."

"How did they know we were coming again, Brewster? I thought you said you'd hidden the tracker bot this time."

"I don't know, sir. I assure you. We did nothing to alert them of our arrival in the area. We used the disguised bot and followed the tracker here. The enclave IT specialist installed it deep in the sub's implant. As long as that is hidden there, we should be able to home in on her location whenever she connects to the Mantle."

"I don't want excuses, Brewster. I want results. We should've been able to catch her the first time we tracked her down. Figure out how she's being alerted to us and cut it off. Understood?"

Brewster nodded. The other two men in the room worked very

hard to appear engrossed in their search efforts and oblivious to the discussion happening behind them.

"I didn't hear you, Brewster. Is. That. Understood?"

Brewster cleared his throat. "Yes, sir, Mr. Cantwell. We'll figure it out. There's no way this girl has the experience needed to evade us much longer. We're definitely closer this time than ever before."

Simon snorted in reply and turned around. He stepped back into the parking lot. He noticed a short woman in her mid-to-late sixties standing just outside the motel office watching him and his men.

He nodded a greeting at the woman.

She returned his nod.

Simon smiled. Maybe there was another way to track the girl and her accomplices down. He crossed the lot toward the woman, broadening his smile as he turned on the charm he could use when necessary.

The woman pointed to the collection of black SUVs parked in the motel's small lot. "What kind of Federal agents are you folks again?"

"We're a special bureau involved with tracking down hackers and their robots who steal information and money from people's accounts on the Mantle. Do you mind if I ask you a few questions?"

"Never did trust that robot crap much. Can't relate to machines the way you can to a person. I'd really like to see Mr. Sterling Noble get elected so he can do what he needs to do. We have to stop everyone from relying on the machines so much."

Simon nodded. This was going better than he'd hoped. If he'd known this woman was a sympathizer, he'd have approached her sooner.

He hooked a thumb over his shoulder at the open motel room. "Did you see the two women staying in that room?"

"Weren't two. It was three — all of them kind of young. There was a tall redhead, a brunette just a little shorter than her, and another girl with blondish hair. All of them had attachments. You know what I mean." The woman screwed up her face and pointed to the side of her face.

Simon nodded. "Did you happen to see them leave?"

"No. As far as I knew, they were staying through tomorrow. They paid for the room in advance with cash."

That made sense. They wouldn't want to leave any credit trail that could be tracked after them. "Did you hear them talking about anything in particular when they checked in? It's vital to our investigation that we catch up to them."

"I overheard the brunette talking to the blonde, after they checked in, about something to do with fixing her or making something right again. I couldn't make any sense of it. She looked pretty healthy to me." The old woman scowled up at Simon. "What did they do, anyway?"

"I'm afraid that's confidential and secret, ma'am. I do thank you for your help, though. It's always nice to meet a woman with a sense of civic duty."

"Like I said, I don't want no trouble with anyone, and I don't like having people with robot parts stayin' here. I know I can't refuse to serve them, but I don't trust them when I see them."

Simon smiled and nodded, reaching into his jacket pocket and removing a business card. He glanced at it to double-check and make sure it was the right one. He'd had several batches of cards made up, using different ones depending on what his cover story was at the moment.

This one was plain white. It simply read, "Agent Simon Murphy. Special Investigations Division." Beneath the words was the generic government circular seal with an eagle on it. Below that was a phone number. It looked official enough and it fooled most people he encountered.

"Here's my card, ma'am. If you think of anything else, or if they return, please call me immediately."

"I'll be sure to do that." She glanced past Simon, watching one of his men exit the room, lit up by the headlights. He carried a box to the rear of one of the SUVs. "You and your men aren't damaging anything in there are you?"

"Don't worry about that. I'll make sure we put everything back the way we found it. All you should have to do is get your maid in to clean up and it'll be ready to rent to the next person."

The woman nodded and smiled.

Simon returned the grin and headed back to his vehicle.

He climbed inside and checked the map on the heads-up-display (HUD) hovering over his dashboard. No new traces had come in since he'd arrived. The girl had gone dark again, mere minutes before his assault team had arrived to capture her and her friend, Shelby Moore.

Who was the third girl? Her description matched the one he had for one of the Moore girl's distant cousins, Ramona Roach. There wasn't much out there on her. Everyone he'd contacted since the search began assumed she was dead. There was no record of her anywhere for the last five years.

Simon knew all too well how easy it was to hack into such things and remove yourself from the databases. He'd paid to have it done for himself. Simon Cantwell was the third such identity he'd created for himself following his time in the military.

If Ramona was as good a hacker as her complete removal from the system indicated, that might be the reason why they were having trouble catching the other two girls. He'd have to rethink his strategy for finding them.

Simon tapped a button on the dashboard, opening up his cell phone connection. A virtual video chat-screen popped up in the HUD, showing a vibrating phone handset.

After ringing a few times, a bleary-eyed James Armstrong appeared in the camera pick-ups at the other end. "Simon, I figured it must be you. No one else calls this late at night. Did you find her?"

Simon shook his head. "They left less than an hour before we arrived. I called to let you know where we stand so far, and make sure you or your wife haven't heard from her."

"We've had no contact, I assure you," James said. "Ever since she escaped, killing one of your men and injuring the other, Faye and I have only been focused on making sure she returns to face up to what she's done."

"Anymore on the internal investigation on how she got away? You know as well as I do it's unlikely she escaped all by herself. My men were very capable. I find it difficult to believe one teenaged girl was able to overpower even one of them, let alone do the kind of damage she did to both men."

"We're trying to be discreet in our inquiries. We don't want to alert any of her friends who might have helped her get away. It had to be one or more of her school friends. We're focusing on the ex-girlfriend."

"I expect results, James. This is a serious matter."

"It's going to take time, Simon. We don't have the kind of investigative facilities the local police do, and we're trying to keep the deaths from the authorities and the enclave's community as a whole. You know as well as I do, if the local police find out there was a murder inside the enclave, they'll raid the whole place and start collecting evidence. We don't want that kind of scrutiny."

Simon frowned and nodded. He understood James's concerns, but could there could be something else behind the failure of the investigation? There was something not quite right about what happened at the Armstrong home the night the girl got away. He wasn't sure James or his wife were being completely honest with him.

That didn't matter now, though. He'd deal with them soon enough once this chase was finished. His primary concern was catching Cass and Shelby. He planned on using the information contained in Cass's implant to discredit the video the two of them had recorded and publicly shared.

That video was the only proof linking him to the execution of the subs at the Sapiens Movement rally several months before. That viral video had done more damage to the Movement than anything else arrayed against them had done in years.

"You can go back to bed, James. If there's anything else I need, I'll let you know in the morning. I don't have to impress upon you the importance of this to the cause, do I?"

"Not at all, Simon. You know you have my complete support.

Cass has brought this on herself as far as I'm concerned. Anything that happens is completely on her."

Simon grunted in response and cut the connection. James Armstrong mouthed all the right words, but there was something that warranted further investigation.

Simon turned his attention back to the task at hand and stared through the windshield at the open motel-room door. Two of his men came out with another load of cardboard boxes full of evidence to take back to the warehouse, where they could do a more thorough job of inspection.

It wasn't much. From what he could see, it consisted of a few boxes of food and a couple items of clothing. He wondered if there was anything there to help him figure out how they were staying just one step ahead of him.

The only answer that made sense was they'd found the trojan horse program. Aaron Benson, the IT security specialist at the enclave, had cleverly attached the software virus to the firewall's security response when he installed it to catch Cass in the act.

Simon had to admit it was a stroke of genius. He'd been skeptical, even though Aaron had assured the Simon that the virus was untraceable.

Of course, there was no such thing. All computer software was inherently flawed. It was one of the reasons the machines were destined to lose. Nothing could compete with the power of the human brain. That was why the machines could not be trusted.

Simon tapped the starter button. His SUV's electric engine hummed to life. Stepping on the accelerator, Simon pulled out of the parking lot, his rear tires spitting up a rooster tail of gravel behind it.

His men could finish up here on their own. He had to get on down the road. Since the girls were headed west, they might stop in or around Pittsburgh. He had a few contacts there he could use to help catch them. They owed him a few favors and it was time for him to come and collect on them.

Once they got another ping on the girl, he had to be ready. He

got the feeling that time was running out for him to solve this particular problem.

____

Chapter 3

____

WHEN CASS WOKE UP, the rocking of the van told her they were moving again. She sat up from where she lay on the backseat, rubbing her eyes, trying to wake up.

Ramona was driving and chatting with Shelby. She'd come in during the middle of the conversation, but it sounded like something to do with their extended family.

A wave of dizziness swept over Cass after she sat up. Something inside didn't feel right. She'd been a little weaker every day since she'd left home. Not enough to alarm her at first but enough that she'd begun to notice.

Cass thought at first it was because she hadn't been eating very much. All implants require additional calories to fuel them. Hers was larger and more extensive than most, due to the damaged areas of her brain it supplemented. She had to eat a lot more than even Shelby did to fuel the electro-mechanical interface. Now, though, the bout of weakness was affecting her equilibrium, causing her to sway as she sat upright. Luckily, it only lasted for a few seconds.

Shelby turned to look over her shoulder and saw Cass. "Hey, you're awake. How do you feel? You look a little pale."

"I guess I'm fine."

"You don't sound like you're fine." Shelby's brow furrowed with concern. "What's wrong?"

"I probably just need to eat something. How did the reset go, Ramona? Were you able to reboot my system successfully?"

Ramona glanced at Shelby.

Based on the look on her face, Cass knew the answer. Her shoulders sagged. "So, no good, right?"

Ramona shook her head as she drove, looking up into the rearview mirror to meet Cass's eyes. "It should've worked, Cass. I've never seen anything like what you've got going on in your implant. All the normal subroutines are corrupted. I'm more convinced than ever it's related to when the firewall's security systems at the enclave penetrated your systems."

"What does that mean, exactly?" Cass asked.

"At first I thought it might be some sort of a virus; a self-replicating worm or something that would've attacked any system breaking into the enclave firewall." Ramona shook her head. "I can't find a trace of it though. I'm pretty good at scrubbing code, and I couldn't find anything. Unless someone has created something I haven't seen before, it's not a virus."

"And yet, here I am, with a corrupted implant and feeling like crap."

Shelby jumped in. "You think your implant is making you sick, Cassie?"

"I haven't said anything because I wasn't sure it was my implant doing it. Now I think there might be a bigger problem. So much of my implant is helping the rest of my body function, that I think the virus, or whatever, is affecting my human parts."

Shelby shot a look at Ramona. "Could that be true? Ramona, you have to do something now. She can't wait for your other plans to set up."

"What plans?" Cass asked.

Ramona turned in her seat, letting the autonomous vehicle mode take over driving duties. "I said I was pretty good at this, and I am. Still, there are those out there who are better than me. If we were close to Baltimore, we'd head back to see Derek, the guy who installed that *Protocol One* file. Everything seems to be centered around it in some way, but I can't figure out how to remove it and reset everything else. I've tried everything I can think of at this point."

"You're not making me feel better, Ramona."

Shelby jumped in. "She's got a hacker friend in Pittsburgh, Cassie. That's where we're going next. Ramona's going to get him to help."

"Uh, I wouldn't call him a friend, exactly. He's just a contact I know there who does a little black hat work."

"Black hat?" Cass asked. "That's illegal stuff, right? It's a bad thing."

Shelby smiled. "Sometimes, Cassie, I forget how naïve you are about some things. Black hat refers to a type of hacker, but it doesn't make them evil or something like that."

"Shelby's right, Cass. My contact is involved with some underworld elements, but he's not one of them. He just works for them. He sees himself as more of a revolutionary. He's a bit of an anarchist and doesn't usually allow himself to get involved with anyone else's problems unless there's a profit to be made. Still, he's the only person I know out this way who can help us."

Cass frowned. "We don't have any money, Ramona, at least, not much. We've been living off what you've been able to supply as it is."

Cass suspected Ramona got her money in underhanded ways, too, and could probably be considered a black hat hacker herself. Still, she'd been there to rescue her and was trying to help the two of them escape. She wasn't going to ask questions that she didn't want to know the answers to.

Ramona smiled and reached back to squeeze Cass's hand. "You let me worry about that when the time comes. I still have to figure out how to contact him. He's a hard guy to get ahold of."

"I'll find a way to pay you back, Ramona. I promise."

Ramona laughed. "Don't be silly, Cass. Foiling those Sapiens

First terrorists and helping to spread the word about what they're doing with that video in your head is the only payment I need. I can always get more where that came from."

A thought occurred to Cass. "What's the plan if we can't catch up with this guy?"

"I don't know," Ramona said, shrugging her shoulders. "We'll probably have to circle back and return to Baltimore and track down Derek there. I don't want to do that since it's so close to your home. It's more likely someone there will recognize you and get word to your father. But if this option doesn't work out, finding Derek might be the only solution we have."

Cass considered the options before her. She wanted to be free of this feeling of dread the persistent weakness had brought on. If her implant failed, so did she.

Shelby must've noticed the look on Cass's face and realized some of what was going through her mind. She climbed out of the front passenger seat and slid in beside Cass in the back.

Shelby reached around and pulled Cass close with one arm. She stroked her fingers through Cass's hair with her free hand. "It's going to be alright, Cassie, I promise. Ramona and I'll figure out how to fix this. And then, you and I can start a new life together with new identities and the assurance that no one will find us."

"I hope you're right. All I know is, I can't go back there. There are things they want to do to me, to all of us. Shelby, we can't let that happen. It has to stop."

"Don't worry about that right now. You're tired. Lay your head on my shoulder and rest some more. I'll sit back here with you while Ramona gets us to Pittsburgh. Then we'll figure out what we're going to do."

Cass put her head on Shelby's shoulder. She reached up with her left hand and interlaced her fingers through Shelby's, where they rested on her shoulders.

She felt better right away. Being close to Shelby always made her feel that way.

Cass smiled and closed her eyes. She hoped this was one of

those times where Shelby was right and everything would work out for them.

The failures so far had been demoralizing for all of them. Cass ran through all the things that had gone wrong in her mind until she drifted off to a fitful sleep curled up against Shelby.

Chapter 4

UPON THEIR ARRIVAL in Pittsburgh a few hours later, the three women found themselves searching for another place to stay, while Ramona went about trying to contact her hacker friend.

Now, Cass found herself unable to be patient any longer. She turned from where she was sitting on the bed. The grimy wallpaper covering the room in the tiny flophouse hotel was just an indication of how desperate their situation was.

She and Shelby had rented it that morning, before Ramona headed out to conduct her search alone. It wasn't initially alarming to rent a room in a place that rented them by the hour. Then Shelby explained the reason for the odd arrangement. Now, every stain of the carpet, wall, and elsewhere caused her to cringe in disgust.

Cass turned to the door for what had to be the tenth time. She tried once again to will the door to open and Ramona to return from her excursion.

Shelby must've noticed Cass's glance at the door. She chuckled. "Cassie, relax. Ramona will be back soon enough. Watch something on the screen. I haven't seen one of these old 2-D video screens in a long time. It's kind of weird how they flatten out the three-dimensional holographic shows."

"I just want to find out if she was able to get ahold of this guy or not. I'm worried about what might happen if my implant starts to fail."

Shelby got up from the rickety wooden chair next to the room's wooden nightstand. She came over and sat on the bed next to Cass. "You don't have to worry about that, Cassie. We're going to figure this out, together. I won't let anything bad happen to you."

Cass smiled but knew deep down that Shelby's words meant nothing if they didn't find a way to reset her implant. The stark truth of everything that could go wrong was evident to both of them, even if they didn't talk about it openly.

As Cass stared at the video screen across from her, the channel changed twice without notice. She shot a glance at Shelby. "Hey, that's not fair. Put that back. I was watching that show. I can't change the channel remotely, because I'm not allowed to open up my wireless connection to anything."

"Sorry, Cassie. Force of habit." Shelby turned and stared at the screen. The channel flipped back to what Cass had been watching.

Cass smiled. She liked this show and had been binging episodes since they'd arrived. It was a top-rated daytime drama that often tried to integrate themes from current events into its content. She was very interested in one of the storylines having to do with a cyber-human boy who was shunned by his family. She felt like she could identify with him in so many ways. She thought the writers must be cyber-humans themselves because of how well they represented the content.

Beside her, Shelby watched Cass's face as the show came back on and laughed. "I don't know how you watch this stuff, Cass. It's so over-the-top dramatic. Seriously these actors are horrible."

"I know they're not award-winning, but there are things about the show that kind of grab you once you watch a few of the episodes. You should give it a chance."

"Nah, that's all right. I don't mind watching it here with you, but it's not going to be something I put on when I'm by myself. You know me, I prefer stuff that's a little edgier in the content world."

Shelby had a penchant for horror and suspenseful slasher films.

Cass had seen a couple of holovids with Shelby, where Cass spent most of the time with her eyes squeezed shut and her fingers in her ears. The stories weren't so bad, most of the time, but the suspense of the scarier parts made Cass uncomfortable. She always jumped when the killer or monster jumped out from nowhere to take their next victim.

Cass glanced at the screen where the time and date showed in the upper corner. She hadn't realized she'd been watching for so long.

"The show's almost over, Shel. I know I've been hogging the screen. I'll let you put something else on when it's over."

Shelby smiled and nodded. She got up from the bed and walked over to where her backpack sat on a chair by the door. She rummaged through it, digging for something.

A key rattled in the door's old-fashioned mechanical lock while Shelby dug through her bag. Cass looked up at the same time Shelby did.

The door opened, revealing Ramona. She darted inside and closed the door behind her, turning the knob to reset the deadbolt before throwing the key down on the table next to the bed.

Without saying a word, the redhead paced across the room to stare out the window.

Cass wasn't sure what she thought she could see. The window hadn't been cleaned in years and the griminess of it made it nearly impossible to see anything on the other side. Besides, their room faced an alley between the neighboring building and this one. There wouldn't be much to see even if the window was crystal-clear.

"Hey cuz," Shelby said. "Storming in without saying a word about where you've been kind of has me worried. Why are you so nervous? Were you able to find the guy you were looking for?"

Ramona didn't turn around as she answered. "I found a way to leave a message for him. I'm reasonably sure he'll get it, based upon what the person I finally talked to said."

"Then why do you sound so scared?" Cass asked. "You act like someone is chasing you."

As soon as Cass said it, Shelby turned to the door, leaning forward to peer out the peephole to the hallway outside.

Cass looked from Ramona to Shelby. Their reactions had her a little frightened.

She relaxed a bit when Shelby turned around and shook her head to Cass. There was no one there.

Shelby turned to Ramona and said, "Out with it, Cuz. What's got you so worked up?"

Ramona shifted her weight from side to side a few times before she turned around to face them. She waved a hand in the air. "It's probably nothing." As she said it, she began pacing around the small room, occasionally stopping to peer up into a corner of the ceiling, or looking behind the few pieces of furniture. She even checked under the bed.

Cass let out a nervous laugh when Ramona finished her circuit of the room. "Seriously, Ramona? You need to stop. If there's nothing to worry about, then why are you acting like we're under surveillance or something?"

"I'm just being thorough. I've got my implant set up to go off if it detects any independent wireless signal not registered as safe and known inside the room. I want to make sure that the owner of this fleabag hotel isn't selling information on his residents to the highest bidder."

Cass shrugged. "Is that really a thing?"

Ramona nodded. "We can't afford to stay in one of the nicer hotels. They require you to register your credit chip rather than paying cash. That leaves a footprint on the system. While I'm pretty sure the identities I have for myself and Shelby are scrubbed clean, we can't take the chance that there's some way the Sapiens First goons are using them to track us down."

Cass hadn't thought about that, but it made sense. They still hadn't determined how exactly they were being tracked. Only through Shelby's persistence in watching their back trail, had they been able to stay one step ahead of the people following them so far.

"It's clear in the hallway, Ramona. I think we're fine. How long do you think it'll take this guy to get back to you?" Shelby asked. "Do we need to pack up and move again?"

Cass was glad she'd changed the subject. Maybe it would settle Ramona down a little.

Ramona walked back to the window as she answered. "It depends on how important he thinks it is to get back to me. I tried to be cryptic about what I needed. No sense putting too much information out there where it might get into the wrong hands. I'm hoping the lack of info grabs his curiosity and he decides to come and find out what it is I have for him to do." Ramona turned around and smiled for the first time since she'd returned. "I told him I had an impossible hacking job for him. That'll drive him nuts."

"Impossible?" Cass asked. She let out a sigh.

"Don't take that the wrong way, Cass," Ramona said. "I just said that to get him to come out of his hacker lair and hear us out. I know there's a way to fix this even if it's not something I can do on my own. Have faith. I promise we'll find a way to fix your implant. If he can't do it, he'll be pissed enough to help us find a solution with someone who can. Whatever it is that's messing with you will be solved soon. I promise."

"See, Cassie," Shelby said. "I told you Ramona would get all this straightened out. Once we hear back from her hacker bud, everything will be right as rain."

"If you say so. I'm just a little nervous about having someone I don't know poking around in my head like that. It took me a while to get used to letting your friend and Ramona do that, and now I've got to let a total stranger in there. Is he at least a nice guy? Derek came across as pretty harmless once I worked up the courage to go and see him."

Ramona shrugged. "I'm not going to lie, Cass. Muller is a rough character. He's not somebody who has what anyone would call normal manners or etiquette. I think he grew up on his own, alone on the street. He learned everything he had to learn in life the hard way. Because of that, I think he expects everyone else should do the same thing, and that's how he treats people."

"Great. Just what I needed to hear." It was Cass's turn to get up from the bed and pace over to the window to stare out through the haze at the brick wall on the opposite side of the alley. Now, she had to let some sociopath come and dig around in her head. Even if he was able to fix things and make her feel better, while scrubbing her identity, she didn't feel reassured.

Shelby walked over and put a hand on Cass's shoulder. "Hey, why don't we all go out and get something to eat? We haven't had anything since we finished up the rest of our snacks at the rest stop last night." Shelby headed over to the door and turned back to the other two. "There's got to be a diner around here somewhere or something like it. Let's all get out of here and get some fresh air. We're all just testy because we're hungry."

Cass nodded and turned away from the window. She smiled at Shelby. Her girlfriend was probably right. She hadn't eaten anything in almost eight hours now. That could account for the way she felt as much as the ongoing failures in her implant.

"I'm game. What about you, Ramona?"

"Sure. Let's go. Staying in this tiny room is just driving me nuts, and I just got here. I left a signal that'll ping me if Muller responds to my message. I can get that anywhere we go, so let's go grab a bite."

Shelby smiled and opened the door. "After you, ladies."

Cass smiled and led the way with Ramona behind her. Shelby grabbed the key and pulled the door closed behind them, locking it before following the other two down the hallway.

Chapter 5

AN HOUR LATER, the three of them had just finished their lunch at a small neighborhood pub down the street, when Ramona sat up straight, staring straight ahead for a few seconds.

She smiled. "I got the ping. He wants to meet all three of us on a corner not too far from here."

"Isn't that strange?" Shelby asked. "I mean, shouldn't he be meeting us in a building or an office or something?"

Ramona shook her head. "This guy likes to stay on the move. The last time I saw him, he was living out of a panel van that used to be owned by a bakery. He'd gutted the whole backend of the van. He added a fold-down cot built into one wall and a complete data workstation to the other. My guess is, he's either living in that thing still or has upgraded to something like it, only newer and larger."

"Why do you think he's upgraded to something new?" Cass asked.

"Because, like I said earlier, he's been doing a lot of work for some people who pay very well for his services. I'm sure he's upgraded his creature comforts in some way since I last saw him. Don't be surprised if it's just a larger beat-up panel van, though."

Cass resisted the urge to groan at the sketchiness of it all. It wasn't like she had many options. Cass was still apprehensive about having this guy poke around in her head, but she was eager to try to find a way to fix what was wrong with her. At the end of the day, she didn't care if it happened in an old bread truck or a sky-rise penthouse. She just wanted it fixed.

The waitress came by the table and pulled a small tablet out of her apron pocket. "You ladies want any dessert?"

Shelby shook her head. "No thanks, we'll just have the check."

The woman typed something on the screen and turned around to face them, showing the price. "Who's paying?"

Ramona raised her hand. "I've got this." She focused on the small tablet with an intent gaze for a few seconds and the screen changed, to a green checkmark with the word 'paid' beneath it.

The waitress glanced at the screen and slid the tablet back into her apron. "Thanks, ladies. I hope you come back again and thanks for the tip."

"No problem," Ramona said. "Thanks for the quick service. We were starving."

The waitress offered a weary smile, nodded, and walked back to stand behind the counter. She poured some coffee for a few of the patrons seated on stools there, refreshing the contents of their cups.

Ramona slid out of the booth and stood up, waiting for Cass and Shelby to come out the other side.

"You said it wasn't far from here?" Cass asked.

"Yeah, it's about two or three blocks away, from what I can see on the map. It shouldn't take us more than five or ten minutes to get there on foot."

Cass nodded and walked toward the door. She stood up straight and set her shoulders back, trying to act at least confident. In reality, inside, she was readying herself for another disappointment. Her expectations were getting lower and lower with each failure.

Shelby must have noticed something in the expression on her face. She reached out and clasped Cass's hand in hers. "Don't worry. We'll figure this out. I promise."

Cass glanced at Shelby. "I know you believe that. I'm getting pretty frustrated, though. Everyone thought it would be fine the last five times we did this."

"It's understandable. Ramona says this guy is one of the best, though. Coming from her, that's high praise. She doesn't doubt her own skills much, and ranking someone above herself means something. If anyone can figure this out, I'm sure this guy can."

Cass nodded as the two of them walked hand-in-hand out to the sidewalk behind Ramona. Together, the trio turned down the street.

Cass had no idea what to expect when they got to the meeting place, but she figured she'd be ready for anything.

She was wrong.

The three of them arrived at the corner five minutes later. Cass started looking around for someone approaching them who might look like they were the hacker named Muller. She admitted, as she scanned the crowded sidewalks nearby, that she had no idea what a hacker would look like compared to other people. Cass suspected he would have some sort of cyber enhancement just like the three of them. Beyond that, Cass was clueless about what she was looking for. She searched the crowd anyway, which was why she missed it when a large motor coach bus pulled up on the curb nearby.

The doors at the front of the bus opened, and a man in a green sweatsuit jumped out.

His sudden appearance startled Cass.

He had a silver implant situated across the middle of his forehead. It extended down over his right eye and across that side of his face. It was one of the most extensive implants Cass had ever seen.

The strange man turned their way and raised one arm. "Ramona? Ramona Roach?"

Ramona turned around, took one look at the man and the bus behind him and started laughing. She walked over to him, shaking her head as she chuckled.

Cass shot a glance at Shelby, who just shrugged and followed her cousin. Cass fell in behind Shelby, as the three of them approached the man and the luxury tour bus.

"Dexter Muller, how the heck are ya?" Ramona asked.

"Way better than you three, according to the message you left. It sounded more than a little desperate, Ramona. That's not like you, or at least not like the Ramona I used to know. Why did you need to see me so urgently?"

Ramona looked around at the crowd of people passing by on the sidewalk. She leaned in closer to the strange man.

"Got a friend with an identity problem that I can't seem to work around. I'm hoping you might be able to help me crack the code that's causing the problem."

Dexter smiled as he shifted his gaze to the other two women. Something about his one human eye didn't seem entirely sincere to Cass.

"Ramona, if you say you need help, then, of course, I'll take a look at your little problem. Step into my humble abode."

He stepped back toward the bus and gestured to the door with a sweep of one arm. Cass noted the cybernetic hand and forearm as he extended his hand to the door.

Ramona nodded and smiled back at Shelby, and then climbed onto the bus. Dexter followed her in. Shelby and Cass followed him.

As she stepped onto the bus behind Shelby, Cass leaned forward and said, "This doesn't seem like the same guy Ramona described. He seems pretty friendly. Why was she so nervous?"

"Beats me. Let's keep our eyes open. Something about this doesn't feel quite right." To punctuate what she said, Shelby nodded to the rear of the bus. Seated on the plush leather upholstered seats near the back of the bus were three heavily muscled people — a woman, and two men. The only way Cass could think of to describe them at first glance was to call them thugs.

As Ramona, Cass, and Shelby settled into a leather sofa, the automated bus pulled away from the curb and rolled down the busy downtown street to some unknown destination.

Cass assumed Dexter was controlling the bus, though she hadn't heard Dexter issue any commands. He could have just as easily sent them wirelessly via his cybernetic implant to the AI controlling the bus, though. Handling automated vehicles and navigation in complex environments was one of the things the Mantle network was created to do.

Dexter settled in a seat across from the trio of women. "Now, Ramona, why don't you tell me exactly what this particular identity problem you're having is. Once we have it all out in the open, I can make a determination as to whether I can help you or not."

Ramona patted the arm of the plush sofa on which they sat and nodded toward the rest of the bus. "You've moved up in the world, Dex. This is a far cry from that old bread truck you lived in."

Dexter laughed. "Isn't it, though? Let's just say I've had a realization about how I should be using my skills and talents. I decided trying to save the world from itself for free was a losing proposition."

"I'd heard you'd started taking contract work for certain individuals and organizations. I didn't know it was as lucrative as all this."

"This is only one of the things that has changed in my life, Ramona. That said, I haven't forgotten my previous life or the things and obligations that went along with it."

Ramona smiled, though her expression darkened behind the smile. "I'd hoped that perhaps the past was going to be left in the past, Dexter. Any unpleasant history between the two of us can be handled later. My friend here has a problem that needs some attention in the near-term. I'm sure you'd agree we should deal with the present first?"

"Funny you should say that, Ramona. I think forgetting the past is a great way to make yourself repeat the same mistakes in the future." Dexter waved to the three thugs at the back of the bus.

All three of them stood and moved to stand next to the end of the couch where Ramona sat.

She glanced up at the three hulking individuals standing next to her and then back at Dexter. "I thought that might all be past history, Dexter. Do you really think this is necessary?"

"Until you settle your debt with me, Ramona, I will not be handling any particular favors for you or your friends."

Shelby turned to her cousin. "Ramona, what's he talking about? What kind of debt do you owe him?"

"It's nothing, Shelby. We'll deal with it. I honestly thought this had been settled long ago."

Cass glanced up at the three enforcers standing next to Ramona.

She turned to Dexter. "I don't understand. Are you going to help me or not?"

Dexter grinned. "I'm not going to help anybody but myself, little girl. I've stopped doing charity work. Your friend Ramona should've known that. I'm not sure why she thought coming to me was a good idea at all, given our history."

Cass shot a look at Ramona. "Out with it Ramona. What history?"

"Ramona, you didn't tell her about our work together back in the day? Shame on you. Ramona here stole a critical project from under me at a time when I needed the work. It set me back quite a bit and put me on a path I wasn't prepared to go down at the time. I ended up tied up with some very unsavory people."

Looking at the three goons hovering around Ramona, Cass had to choke back her incredulous laughter at the mention of unsavory people.

Ramona shook her head. It didn't look like she bought it either. "We were both working on that hack, Dexter. That code and project was as much mine as it was yours. I needed it to break away from my past and build a reputation for myself. I figured you could deal with the fallout on your own, once I left."

"Oh, I dealt with it. I ended up getting myself into debt with some very nasty people."

"You seem to have landed on your feet. This bus alone must cost nearly a million, especially the way you have it fitted out."

"You have no idea what this bus cost me, Ramona. It was far more than the money. I'll be happy to tell you all about it, once I decide what we're going to do about having you back in town. First thing, though, we're going to drop you and your friends off some-where I can keep an eye on you."

"You act like you've been looking for me for a while."

"I've been looking for you ever since you ran off. You're very good at disappearing, Ramona. I even thought you were dead for a while, until some recent chatter over some black-ops channels mentioned your name."

That sounded dangerous to Cass's ears. The only black-ops

channels Ramona would've appeared in recently had to do with her and the escape from the enclave. That could mean he had some connection to Sapiens First and Simon Cantwell.

Shelby must've reached the same conclusion. She stood up. "I think you should let my friend and me off the bus, Mr. Muller. You obviously have some sort of a problem with my cousin. While I'd love to help with that, my first concern is for Cass. We have no quarrel with you and don't owe you anything."

Dexter smiled at Shelby. "I think you should sit down, young lady. I know exactly who you and your friend are. There's quite a large bounty out right now for information about the two of you. I have to decide whether or not I'm going to claim it. My decision will be influenced by how well you follow my wishes. If you are content to sit still on that couch and not cause any problems while we continue on our drive, I won't have to have my three friends here tie you up or any other unpleasantness like that. Understood?"

Shelby stared at the three thugs standing at the end of the couch for a few seconds. Then she sighed and sat down.

She reached over to grasp Cass's hand as she sat. Shelby gave her hand a gentle squeeze.

Cass realized she'd started trembling and tried to regain control of herself. It was hard. She understood what Dexter had said. He was contemplating turning them over to Simon for some sort of reward.

She didn't know how they'd gotten themselves into this mess after avoiding Simon for all this time. Now that it had happened, Cass didn't see any easy way out of it. She leaned back on the sofa, gripping Shelby's cybernetic hand in hers as she stared out the bus's front windows. The city of Pittsburgh went past as they drove along. The whole time, Cass struggled to figure out what to do next before it was too late.

Chapter 6

SIMON CANTWELL SAT behind the cheap wooden desk in a musty motel room outside Pittsburgh. He'd been answering emails for the last hour, reviewing information from several of his contacts. They'd all been scrubbing the online networks of all trace of the damning video taken by the Armstong girl at what everyone now called the Saturday Massacre.

He hated the term. The news media now routinely applied the moniker to events surrounding the death of the seven subs that day. Simon had his own opinions, of course. He'd made an example of them at that rally. It was something that needed doing to start their most ardent supporters down the path of understanding what the coming war between pure humans and the subs would look like.

Now that the video was out there, though, a lot of support had been garnered among the general public. People shared and reposted the video every day, all over the world. Because of that, his operatives were having difficulty getting rid of the video using any conventional means.

Simon growled under his breath as he pictured the many memes that had cropped up of the video, painting the Movement as inhuman. As if the Sapiens Movement's membership of pure human stock were the inhuman ones.

The facts didn't matter anymore. The video had gone viral and had been uploaded in far too many places to be easily scrubbed from the web. No matter what he did, too many people were looking for it, too many people were downloading it, and too many people were playing it all the time, even now, months later.

He grimaced at a surge of pain from his right hand. Simon glanced down at his hand and realized he'd clenched his fist so hard, he'd dug his fingernails into his palm hard enough to draw blood.

Simon shook his head. He hadn't lost control like that in a long time, but the situation was worse than anything he'd dealt with since his time in the army, very early in his career in black-ops. Now he'd been tripped up in his advance to power by two teenage girls and a viral video recording.

Now, all he could do was try and catch them. If he could get a hold of the original video, he had experts who assured him they could provide evidence the whole thing had been faked, and he should be able to convince Cass Armstrong and Shelby Moore to recant their story that the entire thing was real. He had many resources at his disposal. Simon was sure he could get them to confess to anything he wanted them to. It would be easy enough. His time in military intelligence had taught him a lot.

An alert chimed on his laptop. Simon glanced down and grimaced. It was that bastard, James Armstrong, calling again. Simon had been avoiding talking to him since their last conversation. He still thought the man had something to do with letting his daughter escape. That was something else he had to deal with.

Simon would have to figure some way to trip the man up and prove it if he was going to discredit him in the eyes of their leader, Sterling Noble. James Armstrong still had influence in the Movement, and it was important for Simon to tread carefully until he could find the evidence he needed to prove the man's collusion in the escape.

The phone chimed again. With a sigh, Simon reached out and tapped his finger on the screen, accepting the call.

"Simon. It's good to finally get through to you. I was beginning to think you were dodging my calls." James Armstrong had a smile on his face, but Simon could tell it was faked. James wasn't calling for pleasantries. He'd called to check up on Simon's progress tracking Cass and the other two down.

"I've been very busy, James. You know I have many different projects going at this time. Most of them have been caused by things your daughter has done. I would think you would be more forgiving about letting me get things completed in a timely fashion."

"I'm sorry you've been tied up with so much, Simon. Perhaps I can come out there and help you with your search. I know if I were to catch up with Cass myself, I'm sure I could convince her to come back with me."

Simon suppressed a mocking laugh. The man actually thought his daughter would listen to him after all she'd gone through to escape his clutches. That was only true, of course, if James wasn't complicit in her escape. In that case, letting him anywhere near the search would only serve to help warn her.

Simon suppressed his anger. What a fool James must think he was.

"I am quite all right with the team I have, James. I think it's best you stay there and keep up appearances. What is the story you've given to the rest of your community about Cass's sudden disappearance?"

"I've told people she went back to school early. A few of them questioned me about it because they knew I'd decided not to send her back to that place. I've put them off for now, though. Once we find her, that'll get worked out."

"Good, it's important that we make it look like she left on her own accord. That way, when I finally catch up with her and convince her to do what we need her to do regarding that video, we can get her to sound both contrite and believable to the national press when she tells them the whole video was falsified."

"What, exactly, do you have in mind for her, Simon?"

"James, you know I have many methods at my command to deal with subs. That is especially true when it comes to getting them to tell me what I need to know. In this case, I will be using whatever I have to use to get your daughter to recant the validity of that video."

Simon held James's stare through the video link, daring him to protest.

It was James who looked away first, of course. He glanced down at his desk and shuffled some papers around before glancing back up at the video pickup. "I, uh, certainly hope you'll use the minimum amount of force necessary, Simon. That is all my wife and I ask."

Simon smiled. "Of course, James. I'm not a monster."

He paused and waited until James nodded. It was amusing to watch the man squirm over delicate requests like this. James acted as if he had some limited leverage to ask for any leniency for the girl at this point. He was lucky Simon hadn't put him to the question, along with his wife, Faye.

Turning his attention back to the matter at hand, Simon said, "I will make sure to let you know of any progress I make regarding your daughter at the earliest convenient opportunity, James. In the meantime, I believe you have things of your own to tend to regarding Sterling's upcoming appearances in the media. We still have the business of the Movement to attend to, after all."

"Yes of, of course, you're right. I'll be hard at work as always on the business of the Movement. Thank you for keeping me up-to-date."

Simon nodded. "Good, then I suppose we have nothing more to discuss. I'll contact you if I have any information that I think you need to know. Please don't call me again, James. I don't have the time for the sort of distractions that keep me from getting more important work done."

James stared at the monitor for a few long seconds. Simon thought the man might actually work up the courage to push back at Simon's dismissal. Instead, he merely gave a curt nod and reached out past the video pickup to cut the connection.

Simon laughed aloud as the screen went blank. The man was so predictable and easy to manipulate. James was a weak, poor excuse for a man. If he had a daughter, Simon would never have let anyone do to her what James had let Simon do to Cass — in his own home, no less.

As far as Simon was concerned, that was a sign of a fundamental flaw in James. As such, he could never respect the man.

Of course, the girl wasn't *his* daughter. That meant he wouldn't stop from giving his people the go-ahead to get whatever information they needed from Cass Armstrong once she was captured.

Simon re-opened his email system. Scrolling down, he began working on the next email in the queue. It was a response to a query he'd sent out for information on anyone matching the description of the Armstrong or Moore girls.

His eyebrows shot up in surprise. The email came from an operative he hadn't heard from in years. This one was nearby in Pittsburgh. It seemed someone had a line on where young Miss Armstrong was after all.

Simon reread the message, then closed his laptop and stood up. He dug in his pocket for his phone. If this information was correct, it was time to get the team moving again. They might have her this time.

Chapter 7

DEXTER'S BUS ended up driving to the Pittsburgh suburbs where it came to a gated community. After waiting to be let inside by the guard at the main gate, the bus drove up the broad street to a large mansion sitting apart on a hill with a gate of its own across the driveway.

Heading up the long, curving driveway, they all got a good view of the mansion and the grounds. It was the kind of place Cass had only ever seen on holovid programs about movie stars and drug dealers.

The bus pulled up to a large external building that Cass realized was a huge garage. It had a bay big enough for the bus, as well as a dozen other bays for smaller vehicles. A few of the doors were open, revealing sports cars and one limousine.

After they parked, Dexter moved to the front of the bus and pointed to the three women. "Get them settled on the third floor. They can all share a room. It'll be easier to keep tabs on them there."

"Yes, sir, boss," the muscle-bound woman said.

Dexter hopped down and disappeared inside the vast home.

The female thug, who seemed to be in charge, turned to them.

"You heard him. We're taking you inside. As long as you don't cause us trouble, we won't have a reason to cause you any. Got it?"

Cass nodded, and she heard murmurs of assent from both her companions. What else could they do but go along for the ride at this point?

They accessed the third floor via a set of stairs leading up from the kitchen. Their escort paused midway down a narrow hallway.

"In you go," the woman said as one of her male companions opened the door. "Get comfortable. I don't know what Mr. Muller has in store for you, but I doubt he'll make any decisions right away. One of us will be outside at all times, so don't get any ideas. We'll bring you something to eat. There's a full bathroom attached to the bedroom if you need water."

Cass followed Shelby in, with Ramona close behind. The room contained two large beds, a few chairs, and a desk. There was also a sitting area with a small loveseat situated by a small fireplace.

The first thing Cass did was check the windows. They were sealed, so they were not built to be opened. Most homes in this day and age were not made to be opened that way except in emergencies.

Cass flopped down on the loveseat and turned to stare at Ramona.

"What?" Ramona asked.

"It would've been nice of you to let us know you and your good friend Dexter had a grudge between you."

Ramona shrugged. "It was a long time ago. Honestly, I didn't think anything would come of it. I'd almost forgotten all about it, until I realized where we were and needed to reach out to someone for help."

"Well, he hasn't forgotten," Shelby said. "Seriously, Ramona, Cass is right. You've gotten us into this mess. How are we going to get out of it?"

"Dexter's not an evil guy. He's just flexing his muscles to prove to me he's the better guy and that he landed on his feet after our incident." She gestured at all the trappings of wealth, even here in a third-floor guest bedroom. "I don't know what else he could be doing with us. He never had any need for all of this when I knew him."

"Yeah and about all this wealth," Cass said. "It sounds like he's in bed with some bad people. How do you know he's not in contact with Sapiens First? I'm sure they've got a nice price on my head. Lord knows they have the money to spend when they need to."

Ramona shook her head. "I don't think so. Even Dexter wouldn't do something that foolish. There's no dealing with people like that and he knows it. I could never see him dealing with them."

Cass barked a mocking laugh. "How can you say that? You didn't expect him to take us captive either. Plus, he even mentioned there was a reward for me. Simon has put the word out there's a price on my head. If he and my father are closing in and that reward is out there, what's to keep Dexter from claiming the money for himself and just turning me in?"

Shelby came over and sat down next to her on the loveseat. She put her cybernetic arm around Cass's shoulders. "I'm not gonna let anything bad happen to you. Neither is Ramona." Shelby turned and stared at her cousin. "Right, Cuz?"

"I said it before, and I'll say it again. I can't imagine any way Dexter would turn you over for any kind of reward to those people. He wouldn't have anything to do with them."

Cass didn't buy it. "What if the reward's out there anonymously? What if the money is being offered and no one knows it's from the Sapiens First terror cells? Remember, they're supposed to be a secret and no one knows about them. We do, because we recorded the video and I've met Simon face-to-face. Maybe other people might suspect the truth, but I'm sure a lot of them think it's just a conspiracy theory."

Ramona walked to look out the window, then turned around. "I'm sure he's going to want to gloat over catching me. Plus, he'll want to show off everything he has. The next time I see Dexter, I will make sure to tell him exactly what that reward is for and who it's being offered by. I'll make sure he understands the implications of turning you over to them. Even though you both got caught up with me, he doesn't have any animus towards you. Once he's decided on how to settle the score with me, I'm sure he'll just let the two of you go."

"*If* we see Dexter again," Shelby reminded Ramona. "What's to say he hasn't already reached out and claimed the reward? He could've done that via his implant while he was talking to us and we'd never know."

"He hasn't claimed it," Ramona said. "At least, not yet. I've got bots monitoring the reward money on the dark web boards."

"You knew about the rewards?" Cass asked. She felt betrayed. Had Ramona considered turning her in?

Ramona shrugged. "There was no need to tell you. You had enough on your plate with the worry about your implant's reset issues. There was no need to add anything on top of everything else. Besides, the people who populate those dark web boards are going to be mighty suspicious of someone they don't know reaching out and putting up some random reward offer for two girls on the run."

Shelby let out a snort of disbelief. "Seriously, Ramona? You're claiming the people who inhabit the dark web bulletin boards have a conscience or some set of moral values? Even Cass knows better than that."

"Look, think about our situation. Dexter locked us up, sure. But he hasn't cut us off from contact. It would have been just as easy to put us inside a basement Faraday cage. We all can still reach out and connect with the Mantle. We could potentially call for help if we had anyone else we could turn to."

Cass was shocked. She'd been shut down from wireless connections for the last day. She just assumed Dexter had locked them off from all connection to the outside. "Are you sure?"

Ramona nodded. "Everything is there. He didn't filter anything from us. You'll have to trust me on this. In your case, Cass, I don't recommend connecting. We still don't know how Simon and Sapiens First are tracking us."

Cass ignored the warning. She didn't open to the full Mantle connection, but she did open up a routine local net connection just to check to see if she was connected to standard public databases. Cass didn't care what Ramona said at this point. She wanted to check everything for herself. As soon as she let it connect and verified things, she cut the connection. She was telling the truth.

Shelby must've done the same thing. She nodded. "Great. So we're prisoners, but we're prisoners of a nice person, is that what you're saying?"

Ramona nodded. "Hey, it's better than being locked in a dungeon cell with no contact or connection at all."

Cass got up and checked the rest of the room to see what else she could find. They'd left their backpacks in that run-down hotel room, so they only had the clothes on their backs.

There was a large and luxurious bathroom with gold fixtures and plush bath-towels. For some reason, that made Cass feel a little better. Not much, but a little.

Shelby tapped at the open bathroom door and came in as Cass stood running her fingers over one of the towels. "I guess, for now, we don't have anything to do but pick a bed and get some rest."

Cass nodded. "It's not like we have anything else we can do. I suppose I can watch some holo-drama. At least the two of you can connect to the web and the Mantle."

Shelby came over and took Cass's hands in hers. "So far as prison cells go, this place isn't half bad. Maybe Ramona's right and Dexter just wants to rub her nose in his success."

"Maybe. I don't know."

A tap at the door brought the two of them out of the bathroom, as Ramona said, "Come in."

One of the male thugs opened the door, and the other, taller one came in. He carried their backpacks from their hotel room.

"How'd you get them?" Ramona asked.

"It wasn't hard for the boss to track down where you were staying. He has an arrangement with the owner and he had your stuff brought over."

Cass stalked over and snatched her backpack away from the goon. She started going through the bags.

"If something's missing, we aren't responsible," the taller guy said. "They were delivered that way from the hotel guy."

To Cass, it looked like everything was there. She looked up at the guy and said, "Thank you. It's all here."

"No problem. Sit tight. We'll bring up some food in a little bit."

The two guys left and pulled the door closed.

Shelby came over and picked up her pack from the floor. "Hey, do you have that deck of old-style playing cards you found in the bottom of your old backpack. You said your mom must've packed it for you when she set it up for you to escape. Why don't we play some cards and pass the time?"

Cass dug inside her pack and found the deck of cards her mom had packed. Memories flooded back of her family playing cards on trips together, instead of watching the holo-vids on TV offered at the hotels where they'd stayed. As she grew up, she just thought that was a normal activity for a trip. She'd never realized most people now played such games in a virtual setting or using some kind of electronic format.

Smiling, Cass sat down next to Shelby and took the cards out of the pack to shuffle them.

Shelby reached a hand over and stroked a stray strand of hair back into place as Cass manipulated the cards. The gesture brought a blushing smile to her face as she mixed the cards.

Shelby looked back over her shoulder toward the windows. "Are you going to join us, Ramona?"

"Sure, why not?"

Ramona came over and sat down as Cass began to deal out the cards to everyone. Cass smiled as she started to explain the rules for rummy to the others. If they tired of that game, she knew others to try. They might be here a while.

It turned out they were locked inside that room and the adjoining bathroom for almost two full days. Aside from regular meals brought to the room on a tray by one of the three thugs, Cass, Shelby, and Ramona didn't see any sign of anyone else, including Dexter.

Cass was right about playing rummy all the time. They quickly exhausted the desire to play that game, as well as the others Cass knew. They started coming up with other games and activities early on the second day. Ramona and Shelby searched the web for interesting variations to use with playing cards.

Currently, they were trying to see how tall of a tower they could build on the desk using the cards.

The door swung open, catching Ramona by surprise just as she placed a final card atop the tower. The cards collapsed as her hand jumped at the last instant. A groan went up from the three women.

"Ladies," Dexter said from the doorway. "It's so good to see the three of you have found a way to occupy yourselves." He glanced around the room and shook his head. "My bad. I'd forgotten there was no holoscreen up here in these rooms. My folks should've said something to me, but it appears you are none the worse for the wear."

"Dexter, you need to tell us what is going on, right now." Romano's scowl at having her tower ruined added to her demand. "You mentioned something about a reward being offered for my friends. You haven't done anything stupid, have you? You know who is behind that, don't you?"

"Oh, you remembered that. Yes, well, I had seen something about a reward for two women matching their descriptions. To be honest, there were some things about the way it was posted that seemed a bit sketchy. I never gave it that much thought. I don't have a gripe with the two of you other than your choice of traveling companion. I hope you haven't been worrying about that all this time?"

Cass snorted a laugh as she felt a huge weight lifted from her mind. "Just a bit, and sketchy is one way to put it about that reward offer. Dangerous and terroristic is another. You know we're being chased by Sapiens First, don't you?"

"Yes, I'm aware. I figured that out with a little investigation into the anonymous poster of the reward on the bulletin board. When his signature didn't match up with any known hackers, I had a few of my colleagues in the community look around for other places that handle might have been used. It turns out that individual is quite active in undermining the validity of a certain video that's been making its way around the net lately. You three wouldn't know anything about that, would you?"

Shelby looked at Cass.

Cass caught the slight shake of her head. She got the message. It wasn't the time to let anyone else know they were the ones who took the video, at least not yet.

When no one answered, Dexter shrugged. "Oh well, it's no matter to me. Like I said, you two aren't my primary concern. If the three of you will come along, I have something to discuss with you. I think you'll all find it interesting and perhaps something of mutual benefit for all of us can be derived from it."

"What are you talking about?" Ramona asked.

"All in due time. All in due time." Dexter didn't wait for any more questions. He left the door open as he walked from the room and down the hallway.

Cass looked at Shelby and Ramona. Both of them shrugged. They didn't know what he was getting at, either.

Together, the three of them realized they didn't have much choice. If they wanted to know what he was talking about, they had to go along for now. With that, they all followed Dexter from the room and down the hall.

Chapter 8

CASS, Shelby, and Ramona followed Dexter down to the first floor of his mansion. He led them down a long hallway to the rear of the expansive home.

Dexter opened a reinforced steel door locked with a retinal scanner. "Step inside the place where I do all my best work, ladies."

Cass and the others stepped into a room with a large video console table-top mounted in the center. Currently, it was set up to display a complex holographic map of a cityscape, with tall buildings and broad avenues bordering an intersection of several rivers.

As Cass and Shelby moved around the circular display to the left, Ramona went to the right.

Ramona pointed at the map hovering over the table. "You brought us here to see what exactly?"

"It's Pittsburgh. More specifically, it's a portion of the downtown district where a lot of the city's financial services companies and banks are located."

Ramona frowned. "That's nice. Why show us?"

"Because I finally figured out a way you can pay off your debt to me. I have a little job I need done, and I think the three of you together can pull it off in a way I would not be able to."

His request alarmed Cass. "Ramona, we're not hackers. We're not criminals, either."

Dexter let out a mocking gasp. "I'm no criminal. I'm nothing but a contractor who does very specialized work for people with specific needs. In this case, people who are trying to redistribute the disproportionate wealth accumulated by mega-corporations. They want to place that underused wealth into the hands of those who can do a better job serving the community."

Shelby snorted a laugh. "Sounds like something a criminal would say."

Cass nodded. "Exactly. Ramona, tell him we're not going to do what he asks. Tell him he has to let us go."

Ramona met Cass's eyes, holding her gaze for a second before she shrugged. "I don't think Dexter has to do anything he doesn't want to do, Cass. I'm sorry I got the two of you mixed up with this. I didn't I think my past would get in the way of what Dexter could do for us."

Before Cass could say anything else, Ramona turned back to Dexter. "What's the job?"

"It's just a simple little hack that requires some finesse. In this case, I think it will meet your particular skill-set perfectly."

"What makes you say that?"

"I am too well-known here, as are most of my crew. You're new in town and completely off the grid, or at least without any criminal records. Any authorities scanning the network for intrusions won't recognize who you are right away."

Ramona stared at the center of the hologram and pointed at various flashing points of light situated across the grid in front of her. "So these are the nodes you want me to hack into?"

Dexter smiled and pointed at the hologram. As he did, the view zoomed in on one of the flashing white lights. It grew in size until the words labeling the destination stood out bright and clear.

"The Central Federal Reserve node is located right here. I need you to get into the node and insert a small snippet of code I've created. That's it. If all goes according to plan, you should all be able to get in and out of the location within just a few minutes."

Ramona stared at the flashing node on the display. "Exactly what will this little piece of code do, Dex? If I'm going to do something like this, I need to know what you are planning. You know as well as I do, I'm going to have to improvise once I get in there."

"It's just a little subroutine that secretly converts some transaction types so they will divert a tiny portion of their funds into an offshore account of my choosing."

Cass's jaw dropped. "You want us to rob a bank? Shelby, Ramona, tell him we're not going to do it. I'm not a bank robber."

"Relax little girl," Dexter said. "This isn't a bank robbery. It's just a little hacking into the system. You're not going to be confronting security guards, or sticking up a bank teller with a note and a gun in your pocket. This is way more sophisticated than that. I figure the three of you can get it done so quickly, you'll be back and eating a victory snack in less than an hour."

Ramona pointed to Cass and Shelby. "If all you need is a way to get the code inserted, why do you need them? This is something I should be able to do on my own. What aren't you telling us."

Dexter laughed. "You've always been a shrewd one, Ramona. In this situation, your friends actually have some tools that might lend themselves to helping you out. I'm particularly interested in what young Shelby here can do if I get her a few special attachments for that arm of hers."

Cass glanced over at Shelby's cybernetic arm. She had several different types of tools hidden within the fingertips of that hand.

Shelby clutched her cyber-hand to her chest as if trying to protect it. "I like my arm just the way it is, thank you. I don't really want any additional attachments for it right now."

"Never say never, young lady. The things I'm willing to offer you don't come cheap. Do the job, and you can keep them if you want. They might come in handy for you in any number of situations in the future."

Shelby started to protest but stopped when Ramona raised a hand. "Let's hear him out, Shelby. It's not like we're going anywhere right now. I know him. He's not going to back down. This is the plan he has for us."

Cass didn't like the sound of her response. Ramona seemed to be considering hacking the banking system as Dexter wanted. She knew the other woman was correct in saying they weren't going anywhere. Dexter held them captive, and he was only going to let them go if they did what he asked.

"Dexter," Ramona said. "If I remember correctly, the Federal Reserve nodes are protected by both mechanical security systems and software interlocks to prevent hacking."

"You remember correctly. That's one of the reasons I need all three of you. Once I realized what you all had to offer, this job jumped to the top of the pile. I've been pondering a way to crack this system for over a year. Now you're all here, and the solution presents itself."

Dexter continued, walking around the table. "Shelby here has the cybernetic arm with the ability to use attachments that should enable you to bypass some, if not all of those mechanical safeguards without any additional gear. I can help you overcome the rest. I'm willing to upload a customized hacking package to her cybernetic implant that should enable her to work her way through any kind of lock system she encounters."

The hacker moved along until he stood beside Cass. "There's also a particular challenge inside. It has to do with gaining access to the internal software system. It requires some tricky components that I think Cass might be able to bypass. Judging what you've told me about her implant and its integration with her brain, I think her unique neuro-cerebral interface will allow her to use her ocular implant to bypass some of the software safeguards without tripping the system in any way."

Dexter finished his circuit around the table to stand next to Ramona. "Couple those two things with your own hacking skills and this should be a piece of cake. The trick is to get in and get out without anyone knowing you're there. If you trip any of the alarms inside at any time, the whole job is done. The system will lock down until an internal diagnostic sweep is done. That will ruin everything. We can't let anyone know we've stuck the code into the system or it'll just flag them to reset everything."

Cass shook her head. "I don't see how anything I can do with my ocular implant is going to help you out with this. I have absolutely no hacking or coding skills at all. I barely passed the basic coding class in high school."

Dexter smiled. "You don't give yourself credit. Your medical-grade cerebral implant is a new model that has extremely high-functioning systems completely integrated with your biological neurology. I think that when you are given the ability to visualize the system, you'll be able to see a way past the internal safeguards so that Ramona can do what she needs to do."

"You're asking an awful lot, Dexter," Ramona said. "We either hack this node, or you keep us around for what? To be your personal playthings?"

"I'm not an animal, Ramona. I don't need to keep women locked up like that. I need you to do a job, and you owe me one. If it fails and there's no indication you all tanked the job on purpose, then I'll let you go. However, I can offer you more than just your freedom. If you succeed, not only will I let you go and resolve the debt you owe me, I'll also do what I can to fix Cass's little problem with her implant's system."

This is the first time Dexter had mentioned anything about the original reason they'd contacted him. Cass was surprised. "You can fix what's wrong with me?"

"I think so. Like I said, your system is one of the newer ones to come off the rack from the medical industry. A lot of people don't know much about how it works, but I happen to have a guy on my payroll who used to work for your implant's manufacturer. I told him to look into your problem based on what Ramona has told me. I think he has turned up the reason you're having a problem."

"What is it?" Cass asked.

Dexter laughed and waggled his finger in the air at Cass. "I'm not gonna tell you anything else until the job's done. However, the answer is yes. I think I can fix what's wrong with you."

Cass turned to Shelby. "I don't want to do this, but do we have any choice?"

Shelby paused, then shook her head. "I don't think so, Cassie.

Ramona, you've gotten us into a real mess here. Are you sure you can make sure we're not going to end up getting caught by the authorities and locked up? We already know Simon and the Sapiens Movement has sympathizers inside many police departments. If we end up in police custody, Simon and his grooms will find it easier to get ahold of us."

Ramona nodded. "I'm not going to argue with you about that, Shelby. I don't think you have anything to worry about, though. Dexter here is a man of his word and I'm very good at what I do. If he has everything planned out the way it sounds, we just need to follow his instructions and do what he asks."

"Exactly," Dexter said, a broad grin spreading across his face. "I even already have the Federal Reserve node's security guards in my pocket. With a little finesse, I can hack the system so that their work schedules overlap to give us a window to get it done. They'll make sure to wipe the security cameras, installing fresh memory chips I'll provide them. They'll also look the other way as you ladies make your way inside the node's central control room."

Ramona grimaced but then shrugged and nodded.

Cass could tell the hacker didn't like any of this any more than she and Shelby did. However, the hope that Dexter could fix what was wrong with Cass was a strong motivator for all of them.

Every time Ramona had failed to fix what was wrong with Cass, she had lost a little more hope that she'd ever be right again. This changed that. Cass made up her mind.

"Dexter, if you can fix me, then I'm in."

"Cassie, are you sure?" Shelby asked.

"I am. This has got to be the way we do it, Shel. I need to get this thing fixed. I'm not feeling any better and it's only going to get worse, right?"

Shelby nodded and look at Ramona. "We're in. I hope you know what you're doing because we're going to be counting on you to make sure we get out safely, Cuz."

"Don't worry. I got you both into this mess. I'll make sure you get out free and clear."

Dexter clapped his hands together and smiled. "Excellent!. I think this calls for a bit of a celebration. Why don't you ladies join me for dinner? You must be tired of eating up in your room.

"We can sit down and hammer out the details of what needs to get done. Then, I'll take you all over to my workshop and show you exactly what I'm thinking about for Shelby's arm. I think you'll be delighted with the add-ons I have in mind for you."

Shelby didn't seem all that excited. Cass knew Shelby was very protective and personal about her enhancements. She looked on them as an artistic expression of herself and not utilitarian in the way some others might view similar cybernetics. Shelby looked at her arm precisely the same way she looked at her V-tats, playing animated images on her skin over various parts of her body.

Cass reached out and laced her fingers through Shelby's.

Shelby smiled at her and gave her hand a gentle squeeze.

Ramona nodded. "Dinner sounds nice. I'm starving. I know these ladies are as well. Let's go eat."

Chapter 9

IT DIDN'T TAKE Dexter long to set up everything needed for the job. He and Ramona spent the entire day with their heads together on the plans for the hack.

Part of Cass figured, with the amount of time and attention to detail the two seemed to be paying, the job would be easy. Her complacent feelings were dashed when she overheard them, at one point, arguing over which part of the code was going to trip a system alarm that would lock down the node.

When they finally settled on an answer, it wasn't one that made Cass feel better.

Dexter said, "It'll be your ass on the line, Ramona. At the end of the day, it has to be your call based on what you think is the best option at the time."

The fact that a significant part of the hack was going to be left to a coin-flip decision ramped up Cass's anxiety all over again. She didn't have much time to worry, though. Dexter scheduled the job for the next evening.

A day later, the three women found themselves sitting in the dark, inside a black flower-shop delivery van. The plan outlined by Dexter and Ramona during dinner the night before had been thorough, right down to how they'd get away once they completed the hack.

Ramona drove the van with Shelby sitting in the passenger seat beside her. As they drove along, Shelby kept holding up her left arm and extending one finger of her cybernetic hand after another, displaying a variety of new tools Dexter had installed for her.

Dexter had amazed Shelby with all the things he'd come up with to add to her standard tool kit. Now, in addition to two powered screwdrivers and other simple tools, she had things like a universal skeleton key that was supposed to be able to open any mechanical lock.

There was also a special computer port extension that would allow her to jack directly into various types of systems they might find in the Federal Reserve node. That would help Ramona bypass things as she went about her task of placing the secret code into the system.

The only thing he'd given to Cass was a software schematic he uploaded to her implant. It showed an intricate grid system that looked sort of like a map, except that it was the computer program layout, showing all of the ways that the node's security protocols caused feedback loops, and the backups of backups necessary for keeping the system safe.

He'd told Cass, "All you need to do is make sure we don't trip any of these security workarounds. If you can guide Ramona and Shelby through them, then the rest will be a piece of cake. You are the linchpin of this operation, Cass."

Now they drove through the night, down thinning traffic of downtown streets. Cass flashed back to the way Dexter smiled as he told her the whole job hinged around her. The mere thought made a shiver race down her spine.

She didn't want to be the linchpin or any other kind of pin in this operation. She had virtually no programming experience. It wasn't something a person raised inside the enclave learned.

Cass had tried to explain that to Dexter. When she finished, she knew he thought she was just downplaying what she could do.

He kept telling her she'd know what she needed to do when she saw it. Just trust the uploaded schematic.

Shelby laughed. "Cassie, you have the most horrible look on your face." She leaned back from the front seat to rest her hand on Cass's knee. "It's going to be fine. I think we might have fun with this. Dexter seems to have covered all the bases."

Ramona shook her head. "Dexter has told us everything he knows about. But what about the things he doesn't know about?"

"You're not making me feel better, Ramona."

"All I'm saying is, we've got to keep our eyes open and pay attention to everything going on around us. I'm sure there are protocols and security systems in place he was unable to discover prior to sending us on this job."

"You think we're going to get caught, don't you?" Cass asked.

"No, Shelby and I both told you. We won't let that happen to you. We just have to be on our toes. That's all I'm saying."

Ramona pointed ahead through the windshield. "There's the parking garage. That should lead to the access point for the node. Once we pull into one of the parking spots, we all need to hunker down and wait until I get into the garage's security cameras. I need to put them in a feedback loop. Then we can get out."

Cass nodded, clenching and relaxing her hands a few times to try to calm herself. All of the excitement was feeding adrenaline into her system, making her tremble a little in anticipation.

The van pulled into the garage, driving around to the underground section, until they reached the second-to-lowest level. They parked in a nearly empty portion of the underground garage against a wall.

As Ramona suggested, the three of them stayed put in the van behind the tinted windows. She pulled out a tablet and began tapping away on it, staring in deep concentration at what she saw both there and via her implant's systems.

"Ramona, why use a tablet?" Cass asked. "You're using your implant, too, so why do you need it?"

"The tablet helps me visualize things and also allows me to look at more than one thing at a time, so I can monitor not only the security feed on this level, but also the feeds on the other levels while I work out the hack for the video loop. It's important we make sure we're not getting snuck up on by someone coming from either direction. I'm also erasing our entry into the garage on the cameras. No one must see us come and go."

Cass sat back, waiting while Ramona did her thing. The whole thing took her several long, painful minutes from Cass's perspective.

Eventually, though, Ramona smiled and said, "Bingo. Got it. The cameras on all levels are now on a feedback loop. The guards that are watching, as well as anyone else who watches the playback later, will only see an empty garage with no one walking around. We can get out now."

With the engine off, the air had grown stuffy inside the van. Cass was glad when Ramona nodded and gave permission to open the sliding door. Cass breathed in the cool fresh air and slid from her seat to stand outside.

As soon as she stood, Cass's legs grew wobbly, and dizziness swept over her. She clutched at the side of the van to steady herself.

Shelby rushed over and reached out her hand. "Cass, are you all right? What happened?"

"Just a little dizzy. I'm fine," Cass lied. "Let's go ahead and get this done."

"I should've told Dexter to leave you back at his mansion. We didn't need all three of us here to do this. Ramona and I could've navigated through the system map just as easily as you could."

"I said I'm fine, Shel. Really. Let's get this done. I just got a little woozy when I stood up. I feel better now."

From the look on Shelby's face, she didn't believe any of it. After a few seconds, though, she nodded and turned to Ramona. "All right, you're in the lead, Cuz."

"Follow me. Keep your voices down. We don't know if there are any people working late shifts in the buildings nearby. We want to make sure we hear them before they hear us. No one can know we were here."

Cass and Shelby both nodded and followed Ramona down the ramp to the lower level of the garage.

When they got to the lowest level, Ramona led them to the north corner of the garage, where Dexter had said a door led off to the secret underground Federal Reserve data node.

The door was right where he said it would be. The three women picked up their pace. Thirty seconds later, they stood examining the entrance.

It was an imposing steel structure with both a pair of mechanical deadbolt locks and a magnetic keypad lock situated on the wall next to it.

Ramona stepped aside and turned to Shelby. "All right, you're up."

Shelby nodded and flexed her cybernetic hand, clenching and unclenching her fist. She extended her ring finger as the tip opened up, a thin quarter-inch strip of dull gray of metal extending from it.

She slid the flexible skeleton key into the lock, the metal forming into the profile of the keyhole.

For a few seconds, Shelby concentrated as she stared at the deadbolt. She held her hand steady the whole time.

Then, Shelby's pursed lips broadened into a smile. She twisted her wrist, her finger turning the tumblers in the lock.

Cass's enhanced hearing picked up a faint click, then Shelby removed the key from the lock. As the sliver of metal slid out of the lock, it reformed back into a plain, flat strip of metal again.

"One down, one to go," Shelby said as she repeated the process with the upper lock.

"Now for the keypad," Ramona said. "Dexter said the guard on duty tonight would put invisible ink on his forefinger, before he tapped in his code for the keypad during his routine inspection tonight. Cass, you should be able to see that ink in the ultraviolet spectrum. Can you shift your ocular implant and take a look?"

Cass nodded and concentrated on the settings for her cybernetic eye. Instantly, her visual field to changed color to shades of blue, violet, and deep purple. She stared at the keypad, amazed to see four numbers with splotches of black on them. "I see them," she said. "It's the numbers 2, 5, 9, and 0. I can't tell in which order, though."

"That's all right," Ramona said. "We should be able to punch out the code combinations available for those four numbers quickly enough with this little doohickey Dexter gave me." She extended her hand from her pocket to reveal a small box. Cass had seen Dexter hand it to Ramona before they left his mansion, but hadn't heard what he told her to do with it. At the time, she'd worried it was some kind of bomb or explosive.

Ramona placed the square box over the keypad. A display appeared on the backside of the box. She reached over and tapped the four buttons that were now showing the same black splotches Cass saw with her ocular implant.

Ramona smiled. "This will analyze and depress the four selected keys in rapid succession until it discovers the correct combination. All we have to do is wait a few seconds."

Ramona tapped the activation key on the display, and the numbers on the keypad began to light up in rapid succession. In about three seconds, the door popped open about an inch as the magnetic lock released.

"0925," Ramona said. "Remember that. We might need it to get out later. They may have used the same code on other internal locks. It wouldn't do to have security guards having to memorize multiple key codes to get into various parts of the structure."

"Are we sure the guards are taken care of and on our side?" Cass asked.

"I guess we'll find out," Shelby said. She covered the statement with a nervous laugh, then turned to pull the door open.

Cass glanced past Shelby as the other girl stepped inside. A long concrete hallway with white painted walls and white tile floor stretched out before them.

They were in the system.

———————————————

Chapter 10

———————————————

THE THREE OF them headed down the long hallway until they reached another door. Once again, there was a keypad on the wall next to it, along with a single standard deadbolt lock set in the door.

Ramona smiled. "Time to see if I was right about that code. Shelby, go ahead and spin the lock. I'll enter the code."

Shelby extended her skeleton key again and inserted it into the keyhole for the deadbolt. As soon as she opened the deadbolt, she nodded, and Ramona entered the numbers, "0925."

The door popped open immediately.

Ramona turned to the others and smiled. "See. What did I say? This is going to be a piece of cake!"

She turned and pulled the door open, revealing a small room with a large computer console. Wiring ran from it, into the walls and ceiling all around the rack-mounted computer and memory systems stacked behind the console.

Ramona stepped into the room. Cass and Shelby entered behind her, pulling the door closed. It was cramped with all three of them squeezed inside.

"What now?" Cass asked.

"I guess this is where I test out some of these new attachments," Shelby said.

"Looks like we're going to have to cut open at least one panel with a torch." Ramona pointed to the underside of the countertop extending from the console.

"What torch?" Cass asked.

"This one," Shelby said with a broad grin. She extended her pinky finger. Instantly a jet of blue flame appeared, shooting out from the tip.

"I didn't know you got that added. How does it create the flame?"

"There's a small gas canister installed farther up in my forearm. I have enough juice to fuel a high-energy fusion torch that lasts about five minutes."

"That means you need to get to work. Don't waste the fuel. We might need it later," Ramona reminded her.

Shelby nodded and crouched down, sitting on the floor and turning around. She sat with her shoulders hunched under the counter, pressed up against the front of the console so she stared up at the underside.

As she began to work, Shelby talked her way through the process. "If I do this right and pop open the upper maintenance panel from below, it should give us access to the computer ports and keyboard. That'll allow us to access the system."

Shelby paused and the faint light from the torch winked out. She pulled down a rectangular steel panel and set it on the floor beside her. "Done. No one should notice that we've opened this lower panel, and I'll tack it back in place with spot welds once we're finished."

While Shelby worked, Cass glanced at the door, nervous about their opportunities to escape. They were trapped in here if anyone other than the guards Dexter had paid off decided to come in.

A few seconds later, Shelby reached her human hand up inside the exposed cabinet full of electronics. After a moment's concentration as she twisted herself around to the side, stretched her arm inside even farther.

Then Shelby smiled, and Cass heard a faint click followed by a panel sliding back on the top of the sloped countertop revealing a touchscreen panel and old-fashioned mechanical keyboard interface controls.

They were in.

"Bingo," Ramona said. "Time for me to get to work." She began typing away at the keyboard, staring intently at the characters scrolling by on the screen.

Shelby pulled her arm free. "I'll close up this panel down here. Then I'll come up and help you."

It only took Shelby about thirty seconds to re-attach the panel and weld the edges back in place. She climbed out from under the counter as Ramona continued furiously typing away.

Above the keyboard and touchscreen, a holographic display popped up. It showed a complex grid arrangement of circuits and connections Cass found difficult to understand and follow, as the view on the display shifted and zoomed through different parts of the network.

It seemed to Cass that their work was proceeding as expected, until Ramona's smile turned to a frown. The grid scene on the holographic display had stopped moving.

"What's the problem?" Shelby asked.

"I've run into a firewall I wasn't expecting. Muller didn't say anything about this when he prepped me for the job. He was supposed to have the latest security readout on the nodes. It has to be something that's been newly installed since the last update from his source."

"Let me take a look," Shelby said, stepping up next to Ramona. "I have this new direct interface attachment that might help out."

Shelby extended her forefinger, displaying the computer terminal attachment. She reached out and pressed her finger into a port set into the desktop next to the touchscreen display.

At first, nothing happened. Then, Shelby's entire body stiffened, and she let out a low groaning sound as her eyes rolled back in her head.

"Oh, my God, Shelby, what's wrong?" Cass asked.

She reached out to her girlfriend. Shelby's entire body was rigid, as if every muscle had tensed to its maximum capacity. A slight stream of drool leaked from the corner of her open mouth. Her eyelids fluttered over her eyes, still rolled back in her head.

Cass turned to Ramona. "What's wrong with her? I should try to pull her hand out of the plug."

Cass went to pull Shelby's hand away from the port.

"No," Ramona said. "Whatever you do, don't disconnect her. I think she hit the firewall. Some sort of defensive system has engaged against cyber-human intrusion. Right now, if I were to hazard a guess, her own firewall and security systems are fighting to keep the node's defenses from jacking into her implant and taking over."

"What can we do?" Cass asked.

Ramona gritted her teeth as she leaned forward to stare at the touchscreen mounted beneath the frozen holographic display hovering in mid-air. "I'm trying to break through the firewall from the interface here. If I can crack it, I might be able to stop the defensive system from pushing through."

She paused as she continued to type away. When she spoke again, desperation tinted her voice. "It's not working. I can't stop the defenses from boring through Shelby's firewall."

Cass looked at Shelby and then studied the console. She spotted something off to one side that looked sort of familiar.

She pointed to it, tapping Ramona on the shoulder. "Isn't that a retinal scanner?"

It took the other woman a few seconds to identify where Cass was pointing. "Yeah, it is." She stopped her typing and turned to Cass. "No, you can't. I know what you're thinking, Cass. It's not a good idea. That same defensive system could try to hack into your implant as well."

"It's worth the risk. We can't leave her like this, and you said yourself we can't unplug her until we stop the attack. We've got no choice."

Cass squeezed past Ramona to step to the other side of the tiny compartment. She leaned forward and placed her face directly in front of the retinal scanner, lining up her right, cybernetic eye with the interface.

Using her ocular implant, Cass stared into the lens. She'd used retinal scanners before at school. This time, however, Cass directed her implant's internal systems to zoom in, using her telephoto capabilities to dig into the depths of the retinal scanner itself.

Cass wasn't sure if what she planned to do would even work but, after a brief moment of dizziness and disorientation, her view changed from standing and staring at the retinal scanner. Suddenly, instead of standing outside the cabinet housing the node's interface, she found herself zooming along a grid of complex circuitry and software systems.

From her perspective, it felt like she was flying above a cityscape at night, with thousands of headlights and street-lamps lighting up the city below. There was no sensation of air rushing past her, but she had a definite impression of movement.

Not sure what she was looking for at first, Cass tried to remember what she could see on the holographic screen when Shelby first ran into the firewall. She realized she'd seen something like it before, Cass pulled up the schematic Dexter had loaded into her implant's memory core. It was very similar to what she saw now, though it was not precisely the same.

Shifting her view back to the pseudo-cityscape scene flowing by below her, Cass tried using her other senses inside the system to sort of feel around. She found an area that seemed brighter than the surrounding blocks. Much more traffic came and went from the highlighted zone than from any other area.

Cass shifted direction and started that way, but slowed to a stop just short of it when she detected a shimmering transparent film surrounding this side of the energized area. She'd almost collided with the barrier, only seeing it at the last instant.

Looking left and right, Cass searched for a way around the transparent film preventing access. It seemed insubstantial enough that she could probably force her way through, but something in the back of her mind told her to avoid contact with it.

Floating to the left, Cass followed a separate pathway around the perimeter. She could sense a connection to Shelby inside. This had to be the source of the node's defensive systems, the ones that had somehow captured Shelby.

Cass flew along, remaining above one of the circuit "streets" running below. She realized the lights of vehicles she perceived below were really software strings running along the circuits, doing their work. If she was correct, all she had to do was find one of the lights that turned and entered the security node that was attacking Shelby.

Tilting herself forward, Cass flew down lower until she zoomed along above the lighted blocks representing software code she'd perceived as cars and trucks from high above. The blocks transited the circuitry, some turning off here and there to complete their task in some specific location on the system.

Cass reached out with her senses again, searching for one of the code blocks that might be heading into the security node. After a few seconds, she found one.

A small block of code flashed ahead of her, flagged by her internal senses as connected somehow. Trusting her own implant and intuition, Cass sped up until she hovered directly over the block of code.

It was both shorter and narrower than all the others. She didn't know what that signified, realizing her brain's interpretation of the circuitry was an imperfect thing. It didn't matter in the end. It only mattered that this might give her access to break through the barrier and rescue Shelby.

Focusing her attention on the code snippet, Cass tried to remain as close to it as possible, mimicking every turn and change in velocity as it circled the security node's perimeter. She'd begun to lose hope that it was indeed going to enter the node when it jerked to the right, heading straight for what looked like a solid gray wall.

Cass resisted the urge to flinch and instead tried to get even closer to the code snippet as it raced along its collision course.

She was sure she was about to slam into a real barrier and get caught up just like Shelby, but right before impact, a sort of port opened in both the shimmering barrier and the gray wall. It was small, but Cass thought she could fit if she hugged close to the tiny code box.

Her back scraped along the top of the portal, sending a searing pain back through her mind, but Cass ignored it and held on until she made it through the wall.

Cass looked around as the code box slowed its pace, integrating into the other code traffic zooming around inside the security node. She'd done it.

Letting go of the code snippet, Cass let herself float up and hover above the center of the node, while she searched the various circuits and code blocks that represented themselves as buildings and vehicles below her.

Now that she was inside, Cass hoped to find some trace of Shelby to home in on. Following a vague sense of her girlfriend's presence, Cass moved toward the far corner of the node.

Eventually, she reached the outside of what looked like a plain concrete building. It had several entrances that opened periodically to admit code blocks to transit inside.

Cass picked out two silver pathways leading out from the front of the structure to an open area neighboring it. One led to a symbol she realized was a keyboard. There was a red bar hovering above the icon. She guessed it signified a security protocol was blocking access.

She turned to the second icon connected to the other silver pathway into the building. This one led to a symbol of a circle with two vertical bars inside it. It glowed with alternating red and amber colors.

As she stared at the second icon, Cass had a sudden realization. It looked like an electrical socket, and she snapped her virtual fingers. That must signify the input source for the data port Shelby had jacked into. The amber color must mean it was engaged while the red icon was a security alert.

Cass thought the alternating colors signaled it was still engaged in trying to attack Shelby. She hoped that meant there was still a chance that somebody could get inside that way and complete the opening of the firewall. All she had to do was turn off the security alert that held onto Shelby.

Cass might still need to hang out and to help her, since Shelby was fighting off the defensive systems at the time. Following a thin circuit path leading away from the socket icon, Cass backtracked to a nearby circuit structure. It looked like an old rook or castle from a chess set. It pulsed red like the icon.

Turning to look back at the socket icon, Cass saw how signals passed from this structure to the icon. This was where the defensive software was working to hold Shelby. If she could break through the entrance and get inside, she could shut down the attack on her girlfriend.

Backing up across the traffic-filled street, Cass looked both ways, waiting for a break in the traffic. At the same time, she tried to think of how she could break through. As she did, Cass envisioned herself in a sort of armored suit.

To her surprise, she ended up standing there encased in shining metal like a stylized knight of old. She had a lance in one hand and a shield strapped to the opposite arm. Cass overcame her surprise at the transformation as she spotted a brief break in the traffic.

It was now or never.

Cass charged forward, picking up speed as she forced her implant's armored system to use pure brute force to push past the castle's door.

She wasn't sure what she expected, but it wasn't the impact with a castle door, that was for sure. It felt more like she was pressing through a stiff rubber wall. Refusing to give up, Cass pushed harder, straining against the resistance.

The harder she pushed, the harder it became to push against. Cass poured every ounce of energy she could find into one last thrust, with the lance leading the way.

Suddenly the blockage gave way and Cass broke through to the interior of the castle. Looking around inside, she saw the flashing red pathway leading to a small lever set into the castle's wall. There were other levers connected to other pathways. One other was active as well.

Cass realized that one led to the keyboard input. She could turn off the defenses of both input sources at once.

Starting with the one leading to the socket icon, Cass pulled down on the lever. The flashing red pulses ceased flowing and the circuit path returned to a faint silver trace on the ground.

Moving over to the other engaged pathway, this one solid red, Cass pulled down on the lever and watched as that pathway returned to normal, too.

Exiting the castle, Cass stood on the edge of the street and watched as both the keyboard and socket icon turned green. Both access points now had entry into the node's center.

Seeing her efforts had been successful, Cass tried to lift off the ground as her virtual armor melted away. For some reason, even with the armor removed, she couldn't leave the node's surface. In fact, the harder she tried to lift off, the weaker she became.

Not only couldn't she fly back up to return to herself, but something now had ahold of Cass, pulling her toward the center of the whole massive node. Unable to stop herself, Cass was drawn into the center of the node, a massive ball of white light and energy. The closer she got, the more her consciousness began to fade.

She tried to hold out as long as she could, but it was no use. With the last sigh of resignation, Cass gave up trying to resist and let the node pull her inside.

Chapter 11

OUTSIDE IN THE node's control room, Shelby gasped as the defensive systems suddenly disengaged and she gained control of her implant again. She shrugged off the massive headache pain, caused by the system's hold on her, when she realized she'd broken through the firewall and gained access after all.

Shelby glanced over at Ramona and smiled. "I got in. How about you?"

"I'm in, too. I guess Cass did it."

Both of them looked to over where Cass stood hunched over the console at the retinal scanner. Just as they did, Cass let out a groan and collapsed in a heap on the floor. The retinal scanner's interface blinked once and turned off.

"Cass!" Shelby shouted. She ran around behind Ramona to where Cass had collapsed on the floor. She was breathing, but Shelby was unable to awaken her.

"Is she all right, Shelby?" Ramona asked from where she clicked away at the keyboard.

"I don't know. She's alive, but I can't wake her up."

"Well, keep trying. I'm almost into the center of the node. I'll place the code and then clean up behind us. I'll put everything back the way it was. Hopefully, you can get her to wake up before we have to leave. It shouldn't take me more than a few minutes."

Shelby nodded as Ramona went back to work. She held Cass's hand and leaned forward to whisper in her ear, "Cassie, it's me, Shelby. Come on, sweetie, wake up. Please, wake up."

It was no use. No matter what Shelby tried, she couldn't wake Cass up. She tried sitting her up and rubbing her hands and shoulders. She even tried gentle slaps to her face.

Nothing worked.

A few minutes later, Ramona exclaimed, "Got it!"

The tall redhead stared down at Shelby. "I'm almost finished closing up shop here. How's she doing?"

Shelby looked up and shook her head. "We might have to carry her out."

Ramona frowned. "That's going to suck, especially if we run into anyone in the garage. They'll surely notice us carrying an unconscious girl into a creepy van."

Shelby frowned and Ramona added, "But we'll make do if we have to. Don't worry, Shelby. As long as she's still alive, we can fix what's wrong with her."

"What do you think happened to her?"

"She must have run into something while she was inside the system. We'll know more once she wakes up."

Shelby nodded and continued to hold Cass close to her while Ramona finished up closing out the system. She shut down the node's maintenance system, and the security cover slid smoothly back into place on the metal console.

Shelby stood as Ramona bent down to help lift Cass. Together they picked up the unconscious girl. Draping an arm over each of their shoulders, the two women started to carry her back down the long hallway toward the exit.

Shelby grimaced as she reset the final set of locks on the door inside the garage. She glanced over at Cass, where she leaned against the garage's concrete wall. She looked like she was sleeping.

Shelby shook her head. They'd succeeded, and it looked like they'd get away clean, but at what cost? They wouldn't know until they could get Cass some help.

Bending down and lifting her up again, the two women carried their companion back to the van so they could make their escape. This part of the mission was finished.

In the early hours of the next morning, Shelby paced at the foot of the bed where Cass lay. They were in one of Muller's downtown hideouts. He owned the whole building. They were on the third floor where he had a large loft apartment with several bedrooms.

Ramona and Muller both sat nearby, beside a table set up near the foot of the bed. They had laptops open and stared at their screens while they leaned close, deep in conversation.

Shelby stopped and stared at Cass for nearly a minute. She seemed to be asleep, but she wasn't. They couldn't wake her, no matter what they'd tried. A physician Muller had brought in had said she was in a comatose state. He'd brought a device that he used to perform a portable brain scan. It showed activity, but he said it didn't appear to be healthy. When pressed, the doc couldn't, or wouldn't, elaborate beyond that.

Now, Ramona and Muller worked together to attempt to revive her via her implant's local network connection. They tried to isolate the potential damage that might have been caused while inside the node's systems.

Shelby started to ask them for an update. She stopped herself, though. Interrupting the two hackers, who'd been hard at work for over an hour during this particular session, wasn't going to help Cass. They'd tell her if there was anything new to report.

Shifting direction, Shelby walked over to stand behind the pair, trying to get close but not appear to be trying to eavesdrop. Each of them worked at their laptops, deep into a potential fix for what was going on with Cass.

Ramona pointed at her screen. "I've traced back the timeline to where she first entered the system via the retinal scanner. Here's the datastream she inserted via her ocular implant into the system."

"I've never seen anything quite like that," Muller remarked. He glanced over at his computer and tapped a few keys. "Let me see if I can find that same point in the central firmware of her implant. Perhaps we can track down exactly what happened when she entered the node. Something there shut down a few of the major centers inside the implant that interact with her brain. That's why she is not waking up. Until we can reactivate those centers, I don't think we can get her to awaken."

Ramona nodded and tapped a few keys on her keyboard. She cursed under her breath. "Dammit! It all comes back to that damned *Protocol One* file. I'm afraid we're going to have to backtrack and see if we can find Derek, the one who installed that system in her implant."

"Wait, weird Baltimore Derek was the one who installed it?" Mueller asked. He looked back at his screen and nodded, a grin appearing on his face. "Yeah, now that you mention it, this looks like something he did. He's very good at what he does, but he likes to install extra goodies in his system packs that provide additional functionality. The problem is, he gets too fancy. The ones I've seen are almost always glitchy."

"I've never worked with him before, though I've heard of his work. I don't recall anyone calling him out for problems."

"I don't think anything has gone quite this far before. He clearly only intended this to work for Cass, over the few months she was home for her break. It would've been uninstalled as soon as she went back to school. He never intended it to be discovered or directly attacked. Whatever happened to her in the enclave with their firewall, it corrupted the *Protocol One* file system at a root level where it interfaced directly with her implant."

Ramona nodded. "It makes sense. Then, that root issue was further exacerbated when she delved into the node. The *Protocol One* file system was already corrupted, and its defenses were down, so the node was able to bypass it and go directly into her implant."

"But what does that mean?" Shelby asked from behind the pair.

Ramona looked up at her cousin. "It means we need to find

Derek. We're going to have to go back to the university and track him down."

"You're not gonna find them there," Muller said. "He's moved. All the heat that hit the city after the Saturday Massacre made him nervous. I saw a notation on one of the bulletin boards that if people wanted to look him up, they should track him down in San Francisco."

"San Francisco?" Shelby asked. She turned to look over at Cass. "That's clear across the country. I don't even know if she'll survive a trip like that. We'd need an ambulance."

Ramona had turned back to her system and was tapping away at the keys. "We may not have to worry about transporting her in something like that. I've been following the string from the ocular implant's interaction with the node. I think it's possible to disconnect that part of the interface connection. It won't be perfect, but I think I can disable enough of the backlash to cause her various core systems to start back up again from internal backups. If that's the case, she should wake up at least."

"As long as it doesn't hurt her more than she already is, then do it." Shelby leaned forward over Ramona's shoulder to stare at the screen.

"Cuz, I'm doing the best I can. We're kind of playing in the dark here. Everything about her implant is different from its original specs at this point. Derek's *Protocol One* file rearranged a bunch of things to enable her to penetrate the enclave's firewall, the first time. Since then, even more has changed, both after the firewall attack and now with what happened inside the node."

"What she's trying to say, Shelby," Muller said, "is that we can wake her up, but we're not sure what she'll be like when she does awaken. There are significant differences in her implant's system now and we don't know why or what they'll do to her."

Shelby looked over at Cass.

The choice filled her with a level of anxiety she hadn't antici-pated. What qualified her to decide this for another person?

But they couldn't leave her like this. That was one thing Shelby was sure of. They'd have to take the chance.

Shelby put a hand on Ramona's shoulder but kept her eyes on her girlfriend. "Do it."

Ramona leaned over her keyboard again, typing in a few strings of code. She looked up at Cass as she hit enter.

Shelby shifted her eyes back-and-forth between the screen and Cass. She saw code spinning by on the screen faster than she could read, as whatever Ramona had compiled uploaded into Cass's implant.

At first, nothing happened. Then, with a heaving gasp, Cass's eyes popped open and her hands came up from her sides, reaching out as if trying to fend something off, pushing it away from her.

"Oh my God, oh my God, please help me get out."

Shelby rushed to the side of the bed. "Cassie, honey, don't worry. I'm right here. We got you out."

Cass stared upward at the ceiling for a moment as if trying to look at something there. She turned her head toward Shelby. It seemed at first as if she didn't recognize her girlfriend and Shelby's heart sank.

It took her a moment to focus in on Shelby's face, studying it intently.

Then, the corners of Cass's mouth curled upward in a tiny smile as recognition dawned in her eyes.

A wave of relief washed over Shelby. She squeezed Cass's hand and leaned over to plant a gentle kiss on her lips. "You had us pretty worried for a while, Cass."

"For a while? It feels like I was just inside the node?"

"We've been outside the node for two days, trying to wake you up."

"Two days?" Cass asked. Her brow furrowed in thought for a few seconds. "Did we do it? Did we manage to install Muller's hack?"

Muller stood from where he sat beside the bed. "It's installed and already working, thank you very much. I understand I have you to thank for breaking through the final security measures, though no one seems to know exactly how you did it."

Cass's hand drifted up to the side of her head, her fingers brushing across the metallic surface of her implant. "I'm not sure I understand what I did either. Everything seemed so real in there."

She turned and looked at Muller. "So you did what you said you'd do? You fixed me."

Muller shook his head. "I've done what I could. Unfortunately, what's going on in your implant is beyond what I can do. It's like nothing I've ever seen before. We were lucky to be able to wake you at all."

"I don't understand. You promised if we installed the hack, you'd help me."

"I'm afraid you're going to have to go back and find Derek. He's the one who installed that *Protocol One* file, and that's the root of the problem. He knows the base subroutines inside the code he installed, so he should be able to uninstall it and put everything back the way it was. He'll have an installation record and can reverse engineer the process in a way that should undo what the enclave firewall defenses broke."

Cass smiled. She looked up at Shelby. "Well, that's not so bad. We drive back to Baltimore and find Derek."

Shelby shook her head. "It's not that simple. Derek has moved since the incident at the Sapiens rally. Apparently, he's now in San Francisco."

Cass's eyes widened. "That's so far away. How will we get there in time before my systems fail?"

Ramona leaned forward in her seat. "I think I've stabilized what was going on with you physically. It will only be temporary, but it should hold out long enough for you to get to California."

Shelby leaned over and stroked Cass's hair with her cybernetic hand. "Don't worry. We'll figure out a way to get there and get this all fixed. The important thing is now you're awake we can travel there in the van. We won't have to get there with you lying flat on your back the whole way."

Cass smiled. "I thought you liked me flat on my back?"

Ramona laughed. "Seems like she's feeling a whole lot better.

Maybe we should leave the two of you alone for a little while to catch up."

Shelby caught herself blushing, which astounded her. She didn't get embarrassed by stuff like this. She laughed and bent down to kiss Cass. She loved this woman so much.

Muller nodded as he closed up his laptop and slid it under his arm. "Come on, Ramona. We can head back to my office and I'll make you a drink."

Ramona nodded, grabbing her laptop as well. She looked back over her shoulder as she followed Muller out of the room. "I'll make sure we have things set up so that we can get on the road first thing tomorrow morning. We probably shouldn't wait around here any longer. We wouldn't have stayed this long except for Cass's condition. Make sure both of you are packed up and ready to go."

Shelby nodded. "Thanks, Ramona. Thanks to both of you."

Both Ramona and Muller nodded in reply and left the room. Shelby turned back to Cass, still holding her hand as she sat down on the edge of the bed.

"What happened in there, Cassie? When I came back out of the system and saw you lying there on the floor, I didn't know what to do."

"I don't know. I was surfing down the circuitry inside the center of the computer system. I'd managed to disengage the security system that had grabbed ahold of you. All of a sudden, something tried to pull me into the node's software somehow. It was like I swam against a current too powerful to overcome. No matter what I did, I couldn't break free. Honestly, I thought I was going to be stuck inside that node forever."

"Well, whatever happened, at least you're back with us now. We'll focus on locating Derek once we get out west. Then he can fix whatever else is wrong. You heard Ramona. She and Muller did manage to stabilize things so you shouldn't be any sicker than you already are. At least we have that going for us."

Cass smiled and started to sit up.

Shelby put a hand on her shoulder. "Are you sure you're strong enough to get up?"

"Honestly, I feel fine. I'm just starving. Do you think we can find some food?"

"Sure. Let me help you up and get dressed. Then we'll head to the kitchen and see what we can find in Muller's fridge."

Together the two of them got Cass back in some regular clothes. Then they headed out the door in search of dinner.

Chapter 12

SIMON CANTWELL SAT at his desk, searching his email for the latest of the status reports from around the country. Things weren't looking good, as more and more of the public at large had viewed the viral video Cass had uploaded.

He shook his head. If they didn't catch those two girls and get them to recant the validity of the video soon, there'd be no way the Movement would win any seats in the next election.

Simon ground his teeth as he contemplated how hard he and Sterling Noble had worked to advance the cause, only to have it dashed by something as simple as a pair of teenaged subs.

He was about to open up a new report that had just come in from the Florida delegation when his door burst open.

"We have her, sir!"

Simon turned to see his assistant, Carter, standing in the doorway. His broad smile almost lightened Simon's foul mood.

"Where? When?"

"She first popped up in the system two days ago."

"Two days ago? Why wasn't I notified?"

"It was strange, sir. A notification from one of our bots inside the Mantle spotted her. We're not sure why, but her identifier popped up in one of the Central Federal Reserve nodes. Because of the security systems in place protecting the banking system, we couldn't localize it to any particular city, though. There are dozens of nodes all over the country. Then, it was gone, disappearing as quickly as it appeared. We discounted it as an errant signal, maybe an echo of an earlier banking transaction. Because of that, I decided not to notify you."

Carter paused, trying, without success, to hide his nervousness at admitting to that last decision.

"Go on," Simon said after pausing long enough to watch the boy squirm a little. He nodded to encourage his subordinate to continue his explanation.

Carter swallowed hard, then went on with his explanation. "This afternoon, after being offline without a trace for two days, her system went live again. Until now, she's been hiding herself and limiting Mantle access. This time, she reconnected with the central system with full clarity. We have her location, login time, everything. It's like she wasn't even trying to hide anymore. Then, after being live for about two minutes, it blinked back out. I think she's back into stealth mode again."

"Well, don't keep me waiting. Where is she?"

"Pittsburgh sir. You were right. According to the bot's diagnostics, that's where she's been for the last several days. Despite the brief connection to the system, we have a pretty firm lock on her location, down to the city block. The IP address she connected through might even give us the specific building she's in."

Simon smiled. The girl screwed up this time. Whatever made her let her implant's connection slip wide open like that exposed her to everything he had out looking for her.

"Round up the entire team. I want to be on the road in less than an hour. Also, reach out to our cell in Pittsburgh. I want to make sure she doesn't get away this time."

"Yes, sir. I'll get right on it."

"And Carter, make sure you tell them I want them watching the location. They are to be careful and stay hidden. I don't want them screwing up and giving away this opportunity."

Carter nodded and turned to head back out to his desk in the next room to make the necessary calls.

Simon turned back to his laptop. He opened up his email and sent a message to Sterling. He used an encrypted email address that only Sterling would see. It wasn't a good idea to put something like this out in the open. There were too many enemies trying to break into the Movement's communications.

We found the Armstrong girl.
I am tracking in on her to Pittsburgh now.
I will keep you apprised.

S

Simon hit send on the email and closed his laptop. He placed it into his briefcase then stood and headed out to the outer office they'd rented for a few days in the suburbs north of Pittsburgh. People were racing around. The rented space had provided them an opportunity to have a secure net connection with a landlord who was willing to accept cash for a short-term lease.

Within an hour, the landlord would have no idea who they were or where they were going. He wouldn't be able to identify them beyond some vague descriptions of the local movement intermediaries Simon used to handle the transaction.

Several of the team members went by, gearing up in their tactical attire. This time, they were going to make sure the girl didn't get away. Clearly, she'd gone to ground somewhere amidst Pittsburgh's active sub-human underground.

Simon watched the tactical unit check each other's body armor and weapons loadout. He approved of their attention to detail and caution. There was a small chance this was all some sort of trap laid by those who'd hidden the girl. There were those on the other side who'd love to catch themselves a Sapiens First cell.

He bared his teeth. If they thought they'd catch his men unawares, they were in for a rude awakening. His team was drawn from the best ex-military sympathizers he could find. Maybe they'd get lucky and bag themselves a few other subs for the body count along the way.

Simon turned and walked out to the parking lot. A broad hillside full of trees stretched up from the back of the narrow roadway. They'd chosen this location in a small strip mall because the rear of the building was shielded from view of the surrounding roads and structures. No one would see them loading armed team members or any other incriminating details and make an errant call to the police.

Three black SUVs sat waiting as the team loaded all their gear and the technical equipment. The entire assault group had been staying in the office's back room in their sleeping bags since their arrival. It was too risky to get hotel rooms, because of the way the state and local authorities monitored people who stayed in them. His team didn't mind. At least they hadn't had to sleep outside.

Simon placed his briefcase in the passenger seat of the lead SUV and turned to watch the rest of the group's gear get loaded.

Carter came out carrying two large suitcases. "I have your bags, sir. I'll place them in the back with your other things. Is there anything else we need to do before we leave?"

"Make sure the team leaders do a quick check. We don't want to leave anything behind to indicate who we are or what we were doing."

"Got it, sir. I'll go in personally and make sure everything is cleaned up. Do you want me to fire off a localized EMP blast after we go?"

Simon smiled. Doing that would shut down all circuitry for at least a mile radius around the strip mall. That would scrub Mantle nodes of any search queries that might've gone out from his team in the process of their hunt for the Armstrong girl.

Simon nodded. "Do it. But make sure it's timed so that we are well clear when it goes off. I don't want it getting any of our gear by accident."

Carter nodded and ran back inside. Simon smiled. The kid was new, but he was learning fast. He seemed very dedicated to the cause, too. Perhaps it was time to offer him some advancement in the organization. Sapiens First was always looking for quick-thinking, innovative team members to take leadership roles.

Most of the organization's membership tended toward uneducated thugs organized in local cells. They blamed their own personal problems on the prevalence of robots taking over jobs, transferring that anger to cyber-enhanced individuals, too. They were useful in some ways but tended to act before thinking. They often needed a firm hand to manage their penchant for violence and destruction.

The team finished loading a few minutes later and climbed into their vehicles. Simon got into his and closed the door just as Carter came out. He was the last one out.

The boy gave Simon a thumbs-up as he approached the lead SUV and climbed into the driver's seat. He pressed the button to start the electronic engine.

"Everything's set up, sir. I set the EMP for fifteen minutes. That will give us more than enough time to get outside the pulse's radius."

"Good work, Carter. Let's get on the move. We don't want some random traffic jam holding us up and risking the gear."

Carter nodded and pulled the SUV out of the parking spot, turning down towards the exit leading to the main road. Behind them, the other two SUVs fell in line, as they all headed toward the interstate.

Simon grinned. This time he was close enough to the girl that he could taste it. They had her this time.

Chapter 13

CASS SCOOPED up the last of her spaghetti. Muller had one of his people cook up a batch for dinner that night. It was bubbling away on the stove, and the noodles only took a few minutes to cook. Ramona joined them, and the three ladies sat down and ate a hearty meal.

It was probably just her hunger talking, but Cass felt like she'd never tasted anything so delicious. After being unconscious for almost two days, her body was running on fumes at this point. She finished her second plateful and slid her chair back to grab two thick slices of hot buttered garlic bread.

"Wow, look at you," Shelby said. "You're eating enough for an army."

"Well, this is the best spaghetti ever."

The cook, a tall, burly fellow covered in V-tats, didn't look like he was much of a cook at first glance. The food said otherwise.

He smiled as Cass stood and approached him with her plate. "Thank you very much for the compliment, young lady. It's always nice to be appreciated. Honestly, the goons around here have been eating my food for so long they take it for granted."

"Well, they're crazy," Cass said. She waited as he used tongs to drop a clump of pasta on her plate and then ladled more of the meat sauce over the top. "I might just have to swing through here again if I'm ever back in Pittsburgh."

The cook nodded. "If I'm still here, you're welcome to stop in for a bite anytime you're in the area. I'm sure the boss won't mind."

Cass returned to her seat. She picked up one of the slices of garlic bread and dipped it into some of the sauce at the edge of her plate before shoving it in her mouth. She groaned and closed her eyes as she savored the bite.

She finished the mouthful of warm bread and looked over at Ramona. "So, what's next? You said we have to find Derek in San Francisco. Do we have an address for him at least?"

Ramona shook her head. "Unfortunately not. I think we'll have to get there and make contact in the cyber-human underground community in the city. Hopefully someone there will have word of where he's holed up. I hear he's pretty squirrely about where he lives."

"You're not kidding," Cass said. She chuckled, remembering her encounter with the odd little man. "He lived in a sort of armored sub-basement under an abandoned row-home when I met him. I was scared to death the time I went to get him to install the *Protocol One* program. He's nice enough, though. Hopefully, if we put it out there that I'm looking for him, he'll remember me and reach out to us."

Shelby nodded. "That's a possibility. At least we can hope for that. The thing I'm most worried about is how we're going to afford to travel across the country. We've used pretty much all our cash resources at this point."

"You don't have to worry about that," a voice from the doorway said. Muller stood by the kitchen's entrance. "That hack you put in the Federal Reserve node is working better than expected. We were able to siphon micro amounts off of every transaction. It's already starting to add up. I figure I owe you ladies a little something for the trouble you went through to install it. The least I can do is offer a little bit of cash to help you on your trip."

As he said the words, a message popped into Cass's head

through her cerebral implant. She was connected to Muller's local wireless network, even though she made sure to stay off the broader outside system of the Mantle. She'd had to quickly cut off her signal after waking up when she realized she had been broadcasting at full strength. She figured she'd closed the connection fast enough, so she didn't tell anyone about her slip-up.

Muller's local connection was enough for him to wire her the money he mentioned. Her eyes widened when she saw the amount deposited in a reloadable anonymous credit account. It was just over $10,000.

"Wow, that's a lot." Cass looked around. Judging from the expression on Shelby and Ramona's faces, a similar amount has been deposited in their systems as well.

"I guess you're not such an asshole after all," Ramona said. "You still could've asked us before blackmailing us to get the job done."

Muller shrugged. "I never said I was a nice guy. However, I pay my debts. This job is going to make me a wealthy man, and I'm happy the three of you are all right after everything that happened. Consider it a going away gift, nothing more."

Shelby smiled. "Whatever you want to call it, I'll take it. Thanks for the tip, I guess?"

He nodded and pointed at the food on the table. "How was the spaghetti?"

"It's delicious," Cass said. She had her mouth full of noodles again, but she didn't care. She was only now starting to feel full.

"She's on her third plate," Shelby said. "I keep waiting for noodles to start coming out her ears or something."

Ramona and Cass laughed out loud, and Shelby and Muller joined in. They were all still laughing when the first burst of gunfire sounded somewhere outside the building.

"Is that what I think it was?" Ramona asked. She dropped her fork on the plate and stood up.

Muller's distracted faraway look in his eyes told Cass he was checking remote messages or maybe even video. He growled as he nodded and said, "Something's up downstairs. That was definitely gunshots. You ladies stay here while I go to check it out. I have my regular security team in place outside, just in case, and I haven't heard anything from them yet."

Muller left the room as several more pops sounded outside, the noises drifting up to the third floor where they sat near the kitchen windows.

The cook turned down the heat on the stove and placed the lid over his sauce. He reached under his apron and pulled out a pistol. He checked to make sure it was loaded and started toward the door.

Before he left the room, he glanced back at the women.

"Do what the boss said and stay here. He just sent out an all-hands alert. There's a raid on the building. He didn't say it was police. Otherwise, he'd just have us bug out. My guess is it's a local gang trying to muscle in on his business here. It could be something else, though. Don't come downstairs till someone comes up and gets you."

All three of the women nodded as the cook disappeared down the hallway.

More pops sounded.

This time the sound of gunfire was closer. It came from inside the building, and the sound echoed up the stairway from the lower floors.

Ramona shook her head. "That doesn't sound good. I think we need to find somewhere to hide. If they got inside the building, that means whoever it is got past Muller's outer security team."

Cass stood up along with Shelby. The two of them instinctively reached out to hold each other's hands.

Shelby pointed to the door, "Lead the way. You know this place better than we do."

Shelby and Cass followed Ramona to the door and into the hall-way. More gunfire came up the stairs at the end of the hall. Then the whole building rattled with the sound of a small explosion from somewhere downstairs.

Cass grew more and more worried. This didn't sound like it was a small raid. For the first time, she wondered if Simon and his Sapiens First goons had finally caught up with her.

She hadn't told anybody that when she awoke her full system had opened its connection to the Mantle. Now she wondered if all of his was her fault.

Shelby yanked at her hand. "Cass, what are you doing standing there with your mouth open like that? Come on. We have to get moving. Ramona says there's a back stairway leading down to the first floor over here."

"They're probably be coming up that way, too, right?"

Ramona smiled and said, "Muller showed it to me after we got done with the bank job. He was proud of the fact that this place was once an underground nightclub back in the last century. Apparently, there are all kinds of secret passages dotted throughout the entire structure. The stairway is one of them, and it exits on the first floor via a hidden panel in the wall of his office. No one will know it's there until we open it."

"What are we going to do when we get down there?" Shelby asked. "We don't have any guns, and it's not like we know how to use them anyway."

"My van is in the parking garage next to this building. If we can get out the back, we should be able to make it over there. Then we can get out of here. Muller will have to figure a way out of this on his own."

Fear gripped Cass. She found it hard to decide what to do next. She was also still a little weak from not having eaten for two days. The food she'd just eaten hadn't had a chance to get in her system yet.

Ramona ran to the far end of the hallway to a linen closet. She yanked the door open and reached inside past the stacks of towels and tablecloths. She pulled at something and stepped back. The entire rear of the closet opened, shelves and all, leading to a dark passageway beyond.

"You ladies first," Ramona said. She handed Shelby the keys to the van.

"What are these for?"

"I'm going to stay up here and make sure nobody comes after you. When you get to the first floor, you'll find the hidden door into

Muller's office. Before you open the door, listen to make sure there's nobody on the other side. His office down there has a door that opens out into the back of the building. The van is on the second level of the parking garage, to the right."

"Ramona," Cass said. "You have to come with us."

She shook her head. "I'm staying here. I want to help Muller out of this mess. I just picked up an alert on his organization's network. He's calling for more help. That means he's in trouble down there somewhere. It sounds like they're out front, so that means the back should be clear."

Shelby and Cass's eyes went wide when Ramona reached under her sweater and pulled out a pistol of her own. "I'm not as helpless as I appear."

Shelby pointed at the gun. "When did you get that?"

"I've had it all along. I knew who was chasing us. It didn't seem like it was a good idea for us to be running around unarmed. The people chasing us were out for blood."

More sounds of gunfire came from the stairwell, even closer this time. Cass's enhanced hearing picked up voices shouting, and a few groans and screams of wounded.

Ramona nodded at the secret passage. "You two need to get out of here."

More gunfire sounded on the level just below them. They all heard screams and shouting now.

"Go. Now!" Ramona turned around and crouched by the linen closet, taking partial cover in a doorway. Shelby grabbed at Cass and pushed her through the opening into the dark stairway beyond.

Cass stumbled in the darkness for a second then dialed up the level on the night vision function in her ocular implant. Now that she could see, she reached behind her and grabbed Shelby's hands.

"Just follow me, Shel. I can see fine. Put your hands on my shoulders and follow me. There's nothing on the steps, so we need to go slow and get to the bottom in one piece."

"Whatever you say. I'm counting on you to get us there."

Cass went down. There were two landings below their level. One stopped on the second floor, and a passage went off into the distance, leading somewhere on that level. She and Shelby continued downward until they reached the landing for the ground floor.

The wall in front of them had a metal latch on the interior side. Cass worked out how the mechanism unlocked and turned to Shelby.

"I'm going to open the door. Are you ready?"

"Ready as I'll ever be."

Cass ramped up her hearing. No sounds were coming from the other side. She pushed up on the latch and pulled back to unlock the panel.

She peered through the crack. She saw an empty room with a desk and a few chairs.

"When we get out of here and see Ramona again, Shel, I'm going to give her a big hug."

Shelby nodded. "Once we get into Muller's office, Cass, you head straight out the door and keep going. I'll be right behind you. Let's not make Ramona's decision to stay behind worthless by getting caught."

Cass gave Shelby a grim smile and pulled back on the panel. The door came out through a bookshelf sitting behind Muller's desk. She waited for Shelby to come out the door and pushed the panel closed with a click.

Shelby pointed to the door to the outside. "Cass, get going. I'm right behind you."

Cass nodded and ran toward the exterior door. She stopped, opened it a bit, and looked outside. She couldn't see anyone in the alley behind the building. She pulled the door open and ran out into the alley.

She looked around for the garage Ramona had mentioned. She saw it immediately and turned right down the alley toward the parking structure.

Shelby ran right behind her as she ran for the safety of the van.

Gunfire still sounded sporadically behind them, and she increased her speed.

Cass now heard the sound of sirens in the distance as well. The police had been alerted and were on their way. Hopefully, they arrived in time to arrest whoever had started the attack. If it was Simon and his hit team, it would be great to catch them red-handed in an assault like this.

There was no time to wait around, though. Cass and Shelby disappeared into the garage and headed for the safety of the van.

Chapter 14

CASS AND SHELBY left Pittsburgh behind them and drove west into the evening. It was late at night when they reached Indiana heading toward the middle of the country.

They spent the night in the van in a parking lot next to a charging station, staying only until the charger topped off the batteries with a quick-charge. That would get them a few more hours on the road.

It was still dark when Cass took over driving so Shelby could get some more rest. Shelby had driven most of the night so it was Cass's turn to take the wheel.

As the sun started to rise over the horizon behind them, Cass looked over at Shelby dozing in the passenger seat beside her. The van drove itself for the most part, but Cass still kept an eye on the road ahead and behind them. She still wasn't sure they weren't being followed somehow.

Guilt rocked her as she thought about how she might have caused the Sapiens First terrorists to locate them at Muller's hide-out. She was sure something she'd done when she woke up, before she figured out she was jacked into the Mantle, had something to do with it. She should've told someone. They might have been able to prepare at least.

Cass considered telling Shelby about it when she woke but shook her head. Shelby was worried about what had happened to Ramona and the others back in Pittsburgh. She'd had tried to contact her cousin throughout the night while she drove, but was unsuccessful in reaching her.

Neither of them said anything after each unsuccessful attempt. They both knew what it might mean, and it was apparent on Shelby's face that she feared the worst.

Cass drove on to the west. Her stomach growled and she knew they both needed to stop and get something to eat for real. They'd snacked on some vending machine fare from an automated rest stop but that wasn't enough. They needed to get something substantial to eat and find someplace to get some real rest. They'd also need to charge the van again.

Cass checked over her shoulder again, trying to determine if any of the vehicles behind them looked familiar. She still worried about someone following them.

Maybe they'd do better off the interstate. She'd have less traffic to keep an eye on. They'd be able to spot someone following them with fewer cars on the road.

Seeing an exit up ahead, Cass left the highway and turned south on a smaller state road, wending her way across the flat countryside as she entered an area filled with farms and small communities. As she drove through a few of the small towns along the route, Cass noticed there weren't any cyber-humans among the people there.

She worried about how such places might accept people with cybernetic enhancements like hers and Shelby's. She'd always thought people in these places would be sympathetic to the Sapiens Movement. Even though the Sapiens Movement enclaves she knew of were clustered around the larger cities, her father always told her there was strong support for the Movement in what he called the heartland.

Despite these concerns, Cass decided the risk of being found on the interstate made it worth it. She continued driving south on the state road, heading for an older, less crowded westbound highway.

Shelby finally stirred and woke up as they reached another of the small farming communities. It took her only a few seconds before she realized they weren't on the highway anymore. "Cass, where are we? Why did we get off the interstate?"

"I figured we could use a place to rest and recharge the car away from the main road. We're almost out of juice again so we'll stop in this town up ahead. We can charge up and get something real to eat, too. Besides, I thought getting off the interstate while we did that would make it easier for us to hide from anyone following us. You know they've got to be checking the major rest stops if they've figured out which direction we're going."

Shelby thought about it for a moment and nodded. "Makes sense. So where are we going?"

"I accessed the vehicle's map system rather than my own so that we avoided connecting to anything again. It says there's a small town just a few more miles down the road. It looks like there are several places to eat there and a full-service charging stop as well. I figured we could get something to eat and maybe find a motel or something to rest until the car is fully charged again."

"Sounds good to me."

Cass glanced at her girlfriend. "Should you try getting a hold of Ramona again?"

"I tried to as soon as I woke up. I checked my messages and then sent her another text. Still nothing."

"I'm sure she's fine."

"I have to hope she is. She's tough but maybe not as tough as she makes out to be. She's managed to disappear off the grid and then turn up alive again before, though. There's no reason to think she won't pull it off again."

"That's the ticket. Be positive. She'll reach out to us when she thinks it safe. Until then, we have to trust her ability to keep out of trouble."

It looked to Cass like Shelby forced a smile as she nodded to agree. Shelby turned her attention back to the road as they neared the outskirts of the small farming community.

They passed a sign on the way into the single street passing through the town.

Trumbullville
Population 507

Cass took over manual control of the vehicle as they drove through town. A single traffic light in the center of the town marked the intersection with another state road, this one running east-west. A courthouse sat on opposite corners from an old town hall. The other two corners were occupied by a small grocery store and a diner.

Cass pulled over into a parking spot on the street directly in front of the diner. "Let's go in here and get something to eat. I'll bet the food is pretty good since it's the only restaurant in town."

"I'm starving," Shelby said. "I won't care if it's great or not at this point. It'll be good to get out and stretch our legs a little bit, too."

Cass nodded and turned off the vehicle. There was a charging hook-up directly in front of where she parked. She reached out with her implant and connected with it, careful to use an anonymous local connection only. She deposited the charging fee before pulling the plug off the pedestal and connecting it to the vehicle. It would take a partial quick-charge while they ate, giving them enough to get to someplace where they could rest and fully charge the batteries.

Shelby came over to Cass as they took in the old-fashioned feel of the town's main street. A couple of people had passed by on the sidewalk. All of them gave curious glances at the two strangers to the town. Cass noticed no one had any cybernetic enhancements, at least nothing visible. "I hope they don't have a problem with people like us, Shel. What do you think?"

"Act normal. If we don't cause trouble, no one will cause trouble with us. People just want to live their lives, right?"

"Yeah, I guess so."

The two of them entered the diner and took seats at the counter. There was a small tablet propped up in front of each of the stools where they could enter their orders.

The two of them looked over the menu for a few minutes. Everything looked delicious to Cass. After pondering her options, she selected the Hearty Country Breakfast, which included two eggs, toast, hashbrowns, and a selection of sausage or bacon. She tapped in her entry, adding the option to cook her eggs over medium, and hit send at the same time Shelby made her choice.

Cass looked over at Shelby. "What did you yet?"

"I got the hearty country breakfast. What about you?"

Cass laughed. "Me, too. Great minds think alike, I guess."

Shelby laughed along with her. After the tension of the previous day's flight from Pittsburgh, it felt good to hear each other laughing again.

Cass smiled as she looked around at the patrons in the diner. Only about half of the seats were occupied, but it was early yet. A lot of people wouldn't be awake since it was only seven in the morning.

She noticed several of the people were staring in their direction. She wasn't sure if it was because of their cybernetics or just because they were strangers in town. She'd grown up in the enclave and knew what it was like to be from a community where everyone knew each other on sight and strangers stood out like a sore thumb.

A woman wearing jeans and a T-shirt with a white apron tied around her waist came out from the back with two plates in her hands. She smiled as she came over and set the plates down. "Here you go. Enjoy your food. You get into town this morning?"

"Uh, yes," Cass said. "Why do you ask?"

"You ladies aren't from around here and we don't get many visitors down here in the middle of nowhere. Where are you from?"

Cass glanced at Shelby. Her girlfriend took the lead.

"We're heading west. We were traveling from back east and

decided to get off the interstate and see some of the countryside. It's pretty here."

The woman's smile broadened. "It is at that. It's nice to see folks get off the main trail once in a while. We always appreciate getting a little bit of the interstate traffic down this way. Are you looking to stay in town? Maybe you can partake in some of our famous hometown hospitality."

Cass nodded. "Maybe for a day. We need to charge our vehicle, and honestly, we need to rest up a little bit. Is there a motel or something around?"

The woman shook her head. "Nothing like that. There are a few places that rent rooms, though. A lot of the younger folk are up at the state university, this time of year. I'm sure I can roust up someone who'd be happy to rent a few rooms for the night, or is it just one room for both of you? You look like a couple."

Cass blushed.

Shelby laughed and said, "One room will be fine, thanks for asking."

The waitress nodded and walked away. Behind them, teenage boys came in through the main entrance. They were laughing and carrying on an animated conversation amongst themselves. All three stopped when they spotted Shelby and Cass sitting at the counter.

Cass stole a glance over her shoulder at the commotion. All three of the boys sneered in their direction and then took a booth nearby, next to the window. They all glanced at Cass and Shelby then leaned forward over their table in deep conversation.

"That looks like trouble," Shelby whispered.

"I don't know, Shel. The lady with our food seemed nice enough."

"Yeah, but those three guys over there don't look as friendly."

Cass glanced over at the trio again. One of them pushed another toward the edge of the booth until he stood up. The boy was about six feet tall, broad-shouldered, with short, cropped blonde hair. He hitched at his bluejeans, then looked at his friends. One of them nodded in Cass and Shelby's direction. He took a deep breath and headed towards the counter.

"Okay," Shelby whispered. "Cass, whatever he says, ignore him. Got it?"

Cass nodded as the boy stopped and stood at the counter next to them.

"Hey, ladies, my friends and I noticed you two aren't from around here. We spotted the interesting attachments and V-tats the two of you have. My friends and I wondered if you have any other attachments? You know, the kind we might not be able to see?" He followed his question with a leering wink.

Cass suppressed a groan, unsure how to respond to the disgusting suggestion.

Shelby just stared at her plate and kept eating. Cass decided to follow her lead and did the same.

The boy didn't say anything else for a few seconds. He turned and looked back at his friends.

One of the others got up from the booth and came over to join him. "My friend Joey here asked you a question. I think if you're going to be visiting our town, you shouldn't be rude like that. Answer his question. It's just common curiosity after all. We haven't met many people like you."

"Look," Shelby said. "We don't want any trouble. We just stopped here for something to eat and to charge our vehicle. We're not staying long."

Cass looked around, hoping one of the other patrons might help in some way. Everyone looked away, avoiding eye contact with her.

Shelby leaned forward to look around Cass at the two boys. "Leave us be. We just stopped for something to eat. We're not much for conversation and just want to sit here by ourselves, thank you."

"I don't see why you have to be so rude to us," the second boy said. "Consider us the town's welcoming party. You like to party, don't you? We've seen holovids with girls like you. We know."

"Not like us, you haven't," Shelby snapped. Her anger and fear were coloring her tone now. "You shouldn't believe everything you see in online porn."

The second boy, who seemed to be the one in charge, reached out and grabbed Cass's arm, spinning her around on the stool until the right side of her face had turned his way. "Now, that right there is a fancy looking attachment, don't you think Joey?"

The other boy nodded. "Yeah, I wonder how much of her brain they had to suck out of her head to put that machine in there. It's probably why she don't talk much. Maybe she's not smart anymore."

Cass opened her mouth to say something.

Shelby reached out and laid her hand on Cass's arm. "Don't respond to them, Cass. Let's pay our bill and get out of here."

The third boy had come over at this point, joining the other two. They stood in a row now, blocking the way out the front door of the diner. Cass reached out to the tablet in front of her seat and hit the pay button. She wirelessly transferred the money to cover her meal, even though she'd only eaten part of it.

While she paid, the third boy had moved around behind her closer to Shelby. "Hey, Sam, did you notice the brunette here has a metal arm? You gotta wonder if she lost it in some accident or if she had them chop it off on purpose?"

Sam, the leader of the group, sneered at his friend. "Maybe she likes a little pain, why don't you check and see?"

Shelby spun around and held her cybernetic hand directly in the third boy's face. One of her fingers extended, and a jet of blue flame shot out of it. "Careful what you do to me. You might get burned."

She stood up and grabbed Cass with her free hand. "Now, back up and let me and my girlfriend leave in peace."

Sam, the leader, laughed out loud. "Oh boy, Jimbo, you'd better be careful. This girl likes to play with fire."

Cass slid off her stool to stand next to Shelby. The two of them started to veer toward the door. Cass said, "Look, guys, we don't want any trouble. We just stopped to get a bite to eat."

Sam smiled and looked at his two friends. "They're both kind of cute. I call dibs on the blonde."

Joey frowned. "Hey, no fair. I didn't get a chance to pick."

"Don't worry about it, guys," Sam said. "I'll bet these girls don't mind sharing."

Cass glanced at Shelby. She had no idea what they were going to do to get out of this. Neither of them was up to fighting off three full-grown guys, and it didn't look like anyone else in the diner were willing to lend a hand. They were almost to the door when the guys had started coming that way, too.

A voice sounded from the entrance. It was deep and booming. "Do your parents know what you boys are up to? I'd be willing to bet you're supposed to be doing some chores right now, not bothering visitors to our little town."

Cass and Shelby glanced over to see a tall man with graying brown hair standing just a few feet away, inside the entrance.

"Uh," Sam stammered as he and his two friends backed up a step. "Hi, Mr. Cleary. We just stopped in for a pop. Then we were going to head on down the road to my parent's place."

"I think you guys have demonstrated you don't need any pop right now. You can get some out of the machine down at the service station on your way back to your farm. After what I've seen here, I think I need to call your father and have a little chat with him about your manners. We don't harass visitors to our town, especially nice young ladies like these."

Sam opened his mouth to say something, but the man cut him off. "Not a word out of you, Sam. I'm not interested in your excuses. The three of you need to get out of here before I come over there and throw you out."

Mr. Cleary stepped clear of the entrance and pointed out the door.

The three boys walked out the door, their heads down. As soon as they got outside, they ran for a pickup truck parked on the curb. The vehicle sped away down the street, disappearing around the corner.

Cass turned to the man who'd stepped in to help them. "Thank you so much, sir. We don't know what we did to set them off."

"You two don't need to blame yourselves. Those boys are trouble whenever they get together. Somebody's going to have to sit them down and have a long talk with them. I meant what I said. I'll be talking with their parents about this, don't you worry."

Cass nodded, unsure what else to say.

Shelby smiled and said, "Like Cass said, thank you for your help."

"What are you ladies in town for? It's a little far off the beaten track."

"The two of us stopped in to get something to eat and charge up our vehicle before we continued west. This seemed like a nice enough place to stop when we drove into town."

"It is a nice place most of the time. I'm Perry Cleary. It's a pleasure to meet you two. I have a farm just outside of town and a full solar charging array for my equipment and vehicles. I'm a little worried those three boys might come back though if you're sitting around waiting for your vehicle to charge up. If you're willing to follow me just a few miles outside of town, I'm more than happy to let you charge up at my place. Plus, I think my daughter might like to meet the two of you. She has a great deal in common with the two of you."

Cass glanced at Shelby. Ordinarily, she'd be a little suspicious of following a stranger to a remote location outside of a small town like this, but after their run-in with the three boys, she didn't want to stick around any longer than she had to and they did need to charge up the van.

Shelby smiled and nodded at Cass.

She nodded in return.

Shelby said, "We'd appreciate that Mr. Cleary. We're all paid up here, so if you want to give us directions, we'll head out that way."

"I'm parked right outside. If that white van is yours, you can follow me from here. As I said, it's only a few minutes away."

Cass and Shelby smiled as the man walked past them out the front door towards a beat-up old pick up truck. He climbed in and waved at them as they headed for their van. Shelby started it up while Cass climbed in. Hopefully, they'd found a safe haven for a day or so.

Chapter 15

MR. CLEARY'S farm wasn't that far away. Five minutes later, Shelby and Cass drove down a gravel farm lane toward a two-story farmhouse situated in a cluster of trees surrounded by fields. Next to the home, an array of multiple solar panels filled one entire field. They probably provided more than enough electricity to run everything on his farm and then some.

"Looks like he wasn't kidding about his solar charging system." Shelby pointed through the windshield at a pedestal charging station similar to the one they plugged into in town. "I'm just glad he didn't turn out to be a serial killer."

Cass laughed. "I kind of had the same thought, though I'm ashamed to admit it. It was nice of him to help us out back there. We needed to get away from those guys before they decided to come back."

"Definitely. Still, we should make sure we charge up fast and get back on the road. There's a lot of reasons we should keep moving and keep heading west."

Cass nodded. Her problems with her implant weren't getting any better, and there was still the issue of avoiding Simon Cantwell and the Sapiens First teams chasing them. They didn't have Ramona here to keep warning bots scrubbing the Mantle and web of any trace of their passing.

Ahead of them, Mr. Cleary drove toward one of the barns beside the house. He stopped before pulling into the barn, rolling down his window and pointing at the charging pedestal to indicate where they should park.

Shelby waved a thank you and pulled up in front of the charging stand. There were several coiled charging cords hanging on a hook beside the pedestal. Cass hopped out, brought one of them over to the van, and plugged it in. The green indicator light came on showing that the system was set up for a rapid charge. That meant it had a relatively new chipset in the charging pedestal. That surprised her in a remote location like this. She'd have expected a standard household charging setup with a very basic charging system.

Shelby must've noticed it too. "I'll bet he needs the rapid charge to keep his tractors and other equipment running at peak efficiency without losing time working in the field."

Cass nodded as she studied the equipment parked nearby, around the barn and other outbuildings. It certainly made sense. As the two girls turned to walk around the back of the van and see where their host was, they were greeted by the strangest sight either of them had ever seen.

Coming around the corner of the barn was a teenage girl. Her lower legs had been replaced with powerful mechanical steel legs. They appeared to attach to her thighs just below her hips.

To Cass, the legs looked like an industrial robot's appendages that had been adapted for human cybernetic use. She clomped across the farmyard using her powerful legs, as she pulled a wagon full of large round hay bales toward the entrance to the barn.

She stopped when she saw the other two girls standing there watching her and waved. The girl dropped the steering handle leading to the wagon, unhitching it from the towing harness attached to her legs. She turned with a beaming smile spread across her face as she walked over to them in long strides.

"Hi," the girl said as she approached. "I'm Abby. Did you follow my dad in?"

"Um, yeah, we did. I'm Cass, and this is my girlfriend, Shelby. Your dad offered to let us come out here and charge up our vehicle for a while. We had stopped in town for a bite to eat."

"Cool, I'm so glad he did that. I don't get many visitors out here. I don't get into town as much as I used to, either. There's so much work to be done, and Daddy needs the help."

"I see you met our two guests, Abby," Mr. Cleary said as he walked toward them across the gravel of the farmyard. "Sam and Joey Harrison, along with that idiot, Jim, were bothering them in the diner. I figured they probably needed a place to get away from people like them."

Abby rolled her eyes and turned to Cass and Shelby. "So you've met the village idiots, I see. Sorry about that. Most people out here are pretty accepting of people who are different, despite what you might think. Still, there are a few who are more than a little backward."

"A little backward is an understatement," Mr. Cleary snorted in a laugh. "Fact is the Harrisons are a bit inbred, and Jim has never been the smartest of the bunch in his family."

"You've got that right," Abby said. She pointed at Shelby's arm. "I like your cyber parts. That's just about the coolest thing I've ever seen. Do you mind if I take a closer look?"

"No, not at all." Shelby held up her arm as the girl approached a few steps closer.

Her dad laughed and gestured to Shelby. "She's got more than a few tricks hidden up her sleeve, based upon what I saw back at the diner. She's got a butane torch and probably some other pretty cool tools and attachments built-in to that thing, if I'm not mistaken."

Shelby chuckled. "I've had a few enhancements and upgrades added over the last year or so."

To punctuate her statement, Shelby extended the finger with the torch built into it and a blue flame appeared above it for a few seconds. Then she extended each of her other fingers, displaying several different tools, emerging from each one in turn.

"That is so supe," Abby said. "I wish we had an opportunity to get stuff like that out here. After I had my accident with the tractor, Daddy built me these legs himself in the machine shop. They work through a standard mechanical neural interface he had installed at the ends of my legs. It's helped me get around, but they're not practical to go out in public."

Cass smiled and pointed to Abby's legs. "You built those? That's pretty impressive, Mr. Cleary."

"I wish I could've built something a little more sleek and impressive like your friend Shelby has. I was wondering if you might want to stay for dinner while your vehicle charges. I'd love to get a chance to take a closer look at that arm of yours, Shelby. I'm hoping maybe I can adapt some of the things I see there to help improve Abby's legs. I've got a new set that's just about done. I'm hoping maybe with what I learn from you, I can finish them up sooner rather than later. She'd sure like to walk down the street in town without sounding like some industrial work robot tromping along the street."

Shelby smiled. "Sure, Mr. Cleary. I'm happy to help. We'd love to stay for dinner, too. It'll be nice to have something not out of a snack machine. That food back at the diner was the first real food we've had in a while. Plus, if you can look at my arm and learn something about making your daughter's new legs, that's a bonus."

"Good, then, it's settled. I've got to get some work done, but Abby, why don't you take the rest of the day off and hang out with these ladies a little bit? I know you miss having friends around and maybe you can learn something about other folks with cybernetic parts like you have."

"I'm sure we'll find plenty to talk about, Daddy. Thanks."

Cass smiled as Abby's father walked away. "Your dad helped us out back there. He's a really nice man. You don't know how lucky you are to have a dad like that."

"He hates seeing anybody get picked on. Ever since my accident, a few people in town have treated me a lot differently. He doesn't like it when they do. He says that nothing's changed about me and they should act the same way they used to."

Shelby rubbed her cyber hand up her other arm and shivered. "Is there a place we can sit out of the chill. It's getting colder."

Abby smiled. "Absolutely. Sorry, I don't know what I was thinking. If my mom were still alive, she'd be telling me to mind my manners right now. You two go over to the house. The kitchen door's unlocked. I have to park these legs over in the machine shed to charge up. I'll get my wheelchair and be right there."

Shelby and Cass nodded and walked over to the farm house's back porch. They pulled open the kitchen door and stepped inside.

Cass stretched then sat down and watched out the window by the kitchen table, as Abby walked over to one of the open sheds beside the barn. She backed into a docking port so her legs could charge and then lifted herself up using a bar that hung down from the ceiling.

Her legs ended in stumps about halfway between her knees and hips. A metal mechanical interface socket capped the stumps.

Abby used the overhead bar and moved hand-over-hand across it until she lowered herself into a wheelchair sitting next to the docking port. She rolled across the farmyard in their direction with a big grin on her face.

Abby came up the ramp beside the steps onto the porch, then came into the kitchen. She parked herself next to the chair where Cass sat. "Are you two thirsty or hungry?"

Cass shrugged. "I guess maybe a little thirsty. You don't have to get it for me. Just tell me where to look. I can get something for you, too."

"Oh, don't worry about that, Mabel can get it for us." Abby raised her voice and shouted toward the center of the house. "Mabel, bring us three lemonades, please."

The sound of movement in another room down the hallway made Cass was the first sign of someone else in the home.

Shelby asked, "Who's Mabel? Is she a cousin or a maid or something?"

Abby grinned from ear to ear. "You'll see."

As if to punctuate her words, a 7-foot-tall robotic figure came down the hallway into the kitchen.

Cass had seen a lot of robots around the city when she'd moved there for school. This one was unlike any she'd ever seen before. Some robots were built to look vaguely humanoid. They stood on two feet. Those robots were manufactured by one of several companies with a finished appearance.

This robot was built of spare parts from a variety of different pieces of equipment and robots. It rolled along on a double-tread base, leading up to a trunk with four arms, two with cybernetic hands and two with claw-like appendages.

The robot, Mabel, headed to the refrigerator where it filled three glasses with ice, then poured lemonade into each. It turned and brought the three drinks over to the table.

After the tall robot set one of the glasses by each of the women, it stood erect again and said in a warm motherly voice, "Do you need anything else, Abby?"

"No, Mabel. That will be all. Thanks so much."

"You're welcome, dear. Holler if you need anything. I'll be in the other room doing the cleaning."

The robot turned and went back down the hallway, disappearing into the rest of the house.

Abby turned to see Shelby and Cass's expressions at seeing the robot. "You two look hilarious." Abby laughed. She leaned forward in her wheelchair to take a sip from her glass. "Daddy built Mabel soon after Mama died. He figured I needed someone around to keep me straight and help out around the house with chores, since I wasn't up to it after my accident."

"What happened, if you don't mind me asking?" Cass asked.

"Oh, I don't mind. It was six years ago. I was ten and helping out around the farm. I was with my mom while she drove one of the tractors out to the field to pick up a wagon filled with hay bales, ready to come in. I was along to help hitch up the wagon while Mom backed up to it. On the way back in from the field, Mom hit a sinkhole, and the tractor rolled over. I was riding on the wagon. It pitched forward into the hole, and I fell beneath the tractor. It pinned my legs in place and crushed them pretty bad. My mother was thrown from the seat and died later at the hospital from her injuries."

Abby's eyes turn sad. She looked out the window into the fields with a faraway look in her eyes.

"Abby, I'm so sorry." Cass reached out to lay a hand on the girl's arm. "I didn't mean to bring up bad memories."

"It's all right," Abby said with a shrug. "As I said, it was a while ago. I still miss my mom, but Dad does his best to make up for it, and with Mabel around, it's not so lonely."

Cass wasn't sure a robot counted as company, but she wasn't going to say anything. People lived the lives they lived and got used to all sorts of things in the course of everyday living.

From her standpoint, this was just another example of how robotics and cybernetics were good for people. It was so unlike what she'd been taught while being raised in the enclave.

Shelby pointed to the stumps of Abby's legs. "The sockets at the end of your legs look pretty standard. Has your dad ever looked into taking you into a city like Indianapolis and getting some modern cybernetics added? It wouldn't be hard to fit you for them. Then you'd be able to walk around like normal."

"Things are pretty tough here on the farm. Dad does his best with what we have in the machine shop, and he's cobbled together a pretty good cybernetics lab in there, too. We can't afford as much as some people can. It's pretty much up to us to make do with what we can find here on the farm."

Cass realized how different things must be out here where they didn't have access to all the same technologies and advantages she'd grown up with, even in the enclave's tech-phobic community. Judging from the look on Shelby's face, she was having similar thoughts.

"Well if your dad can learn anything from my arm to help him make you better legs, I'm happy to help out. I know a little bit about cybernetics programming. I'm not an expert by any stretch, but I bet I can help point him in the right direction for some new things that might help him out."

Abby smiled. "That would be nice. I'm happy enough with those he's already built me. But something to wear into town would be nice. The other ones are the kind of thing you need on a farm like this. I could never pull a wagon by myself without them. They make me a lot more useful around the farm than I would be even if I had my real legs."

"You certainly have a good attitude about it," Cass said. "I know when I had my accident, I wasn't quite so accepting of my new additions."

Abby stared at the side of Cass's head where her implant ran from just above her cheek across to her ear. "I saw that you had an implant. Shelby's enhancements are pretty obvious. Between her V-tats and the arm, it's clear she's had some work done. Other than the implant in the side of your head, though, I can't tell what kind of work you had done."

Cass reached up to pull her hair down over the implant, still self-conscious about it. She stopped herself and put her hand down to rest in her lap.

She smiled at Abby. "It's pretty cool. I have a cybernetic eye that lets me see in the dark and some other cool stuff. My right ear is also cybernetic, so I can hear things most people can't hear from far away and stuff like that."

"That's pretty awesome. That's the kind of thing that you read about in stories."

Cass shrugged. "It's not something I would've asked for before the accident. I hit my head while on vacation. They had to put the implant in to keep me alive. I've gotten pretty used to it at this point, though. I hardly even notice it's there anymore."

Abby smiled. "It's funny what you get used to after a while, isn't it?"

Shelby said, "Everybody has their own life to live. It doesn't pay to get too upset about it when life tosses you a curveball. If life gives you something hard to deal with, you either deal with it, or you roll over and die."

Abby nodded.

The three of them sat for a while in silence and sipped at their lemonade looking out the window.

Cass realized this was a welcome break from being on the run. She wondered if they could stay here for longer than just the afternoon. She'd have to talk to Shelby about it. These were friendly people, and she'd enjoy getting to know them better. Plus it would be nice to stop and gather themselves with a plan before heading out to San Francisco again.

Chapter 16

SIMON STARED at the email for several minutes, trying to make up his mind on what to do about it. He'd lost too many men in the raid on that damned building in Pittsburgh and had nothing to show for it.

The place turned out to be a fortified hideout for some sub-human underworld figure. No one had bothered to check beforehand, and they'd walked into a bloodbath.

His men killed a few subs along the way, but once the element of surprise passed, the subs in the building had been more than capable of defending themselves from his assault. On top of that, it appeared both the Armstrong girl and Shelby Moore had been there, but still managed to escape.

Now he had fewer people at his disposal. The intact teams he had left were split up and spread out in all directions, searching for any trace of which way the two of them went after escaping.

They'd been gone for more than twenty-four hours at this point and he knew with every passing minute the trail got even colder. He'd had numerous reports in from various sources, some reported to be reliable, others not so much.

He'd had to send somebody to check out each one. Now a

person sympathetic to the cause had sent an email to one of his contacts with a grainy photograph taken from social media that looked like two girls squaring off with a few boys in some midwestern town south of Indianapolis.

There was no reason at all for either of the girls to be there. He could find no family or friend connections to the area. He also couldn't reason why they would be off the main thoroughfares.

After pondering the email a little longer, Simon decided to send the only team he had left to check on it, just in case.

"Carter, get in here."

His assistant came in from the outer room of the hotel suite they now shared. This served as their office since getting to Pittsburgh. He rarely got a chance to live in relative comfort and had decided to stay here in the popular hotel chain until they had a solid lead on which way the two fugitives had gone.

Carter came in and stood next to the table Simon had been using as his desk. "What is it, sir?"

"Have you seen this email from the contact in Indiana?"

Carter nodded. "It seems a bit sketchy, sir. I almost didn't forward it to you, but your instructions were clear. I can't find any connection for either girl to the place."

"That was my thought exactly. I'm concerned, though, that we still haven't found them on the normal westward routes. I fear we still have to follow up on it. Do we have the name of the contact who sent in the photograph?"

"I don't have it on me. However, I can look it up and get it."

"Good. Figure out who it is. Then pull together a team and send them out that way to check on it. Tell them if the contact seems unsure at all, to mark it off and come back."

Carter shrugged and paused before answering.

"Is there a problem, Carter?"

"It's just that we're spread very thin, as I'm sure you are aware. The only people we have left are from your security team. If we send them, there'll be nobody left here holding down the fort except for you and me."

"I'm aware of the danger. However, no one is looking for me, and we need boots on the ground. Send off the three of them to check out that place in Indiana. They'll either track down the girls or come back. Worst case scenario, they're gone for a day and a half, maybe two. Either way, we'll find out what we need to find out. If you're concerned about security, I have a contact in the local police force. You have my permission to hire some off-duty officers to keep watch until the team returns."

Carter nodded. "Very well, Mr. Cantwell. I'll get right on it."

The assistant turned and headed back into the other room.

Simon watched him leave. His instincts about the boy were on-target. It was good he wasn't so afraid of Simon that he wasn't willing to share concerns and doubts about things his boss considered. That was rare in an underling. Simon decided he'd reward him sooner rather than later. That probably meant giving him a team of his own in some form, but at least he'd be able to keep Carter under his influence as a team leader.

Simon sighed. It was so difficult to find decent help these days.

He turned back to his computer, scrolling down the screen at other random sightings of the two girls. It had been touchy sending out requests for information without alerting any of the authorities who might be tracking down the increased rumors of Sapiens First activity around the country.

While the general public thought the tactical arm of the Sapiens Movement was an urban myth, Simon knew some Federal agents were trying to pin the Saturday Massacre on and him and his team.

So far, they'd had no direct evidence of the accuracy of the viral video. If Simon had anything to say about it, they never would. Still, he hadn't reached his position without being pragmatic about the chances it all might turn against him.

The more he thought about it, the more he decided it might make sense for him to make sure his personal contingency plan for escape was in place. While he generally espoused the ideals held by Sterling Noble and others in the movement, Simon had his own agenda and wouldn't allow himself to be caught up in anything that implicated the candidate or anyone who followed him. Simon had survived on his own this long in one identity or another, and he'd figure out a way to get out of this, too, if things fell apart for this persona.

Opening up another screen, Simon checked a secret bank account he maintained in the Caribbean. He'd been siphoning off small amounts of the money Sapiens First received from the central organization for almost two years. His little nest egg had grown quite a bit. It was already enough for him to live the rest of his life in relative comfort on some tropical beach.

Simon checked the figures and latest deposits and investments one last time. For a brief instant, he considered closing up the operation and going dark. He had several options for his next identity already in place. All he had to do was make a few phone calls and walk away from all of this.

He looked down at the total balance in his account. As long as the search for the two girls went on, he could dig deep into the money trough that fed his efforts. That meant there was even more to send through to his private accounts. If the search continued for even a few more weeks, he could add another fifty percent to his balance.

That final calculation decided it for him. He'd complete the search for the two girls, finish the mission at hand, then silently disappear. If Sterling or any of the other leaders in the movement tried to come after him, he'd send them a copy of all the evidence against each of them he'd collected over the last few years. He was sure none of them had the stomach to call his bluff.

Closing the account screen, Simon went back to reviewing his emails and figuring ways he could increase his expenditures for the search even more.

Chapter 17

CASS AND SHELBY ended up staying and enjoying an additional day on the Cleary farm. Both Mr. Cleary and Abby were wonderful, happy to open up their home to the two visitors. Shelby spent a good deal of time with Mr. Cleary the evening they arrived, working in his cybernetics machine shop, talking about her cyber-arm and about ways he might be able to streamline appendages he could devise for his daughter's use.

Cass spent the time talking with Abby and walking around the farm, helping with some of the late afternoon chores. It was a pleasant evening and an even better day the beginning of the following morning.

Both Shelby and Cass lent a hand doing some of the chores, with Abby showing them what to do. Neither of the two had ever done work like this before in their lives. However, to Cass, there was something about it that made her feel good. She got a glimpse about how working with the land on a farm like this could be so satisfying.

As Cass sat down to dinner on the second day, she realized she was both hungry and exhausted. Both felt good to her, though. It was a good kind of tired and the type of hunger that came from a hard day's work. The hearty meal in front of them would more than fill her belly.

"Abby, when you're done with those potatoes, could you pass them my way?" Cass asked.

"Sure. I'm done." Abby put the spoon back in the bowl of mashed potatoes and passed it across the table to Cass before picking up the gravy boat and ladling some fresh brown gravy over the mound of fluffy potatoes. The meal of steak, mashed potatoes, fresh green beans, and a fruit salad was delicious. Each of them was on their second helping at this point.

A signal chimed from Mr. Cleary's pocket. He pulled out his phone and glanced at the screen. "That's strange."

"What is it, Daddy?"

"Just got a message from Matilda at the diner in town. She says to call her right away."

"Oh, she's probably having a problem with that robot chef again. She wants an excuse to have you come into town since you're the only eligible bachelor her age around."

Mr. Cleary laughed and shook his head. "Abby, it's about time you stop trying to marry me off to every single woman in the area. I still miss your mother a lot, and for now, I'm not looking for more."

"Hey, a girl's got to help her single dad out when he needs it."

Cass smiled at the casual by-play between the two of them. Though the pain of Abby's mother's death still registered in both of them, they'd reached a sort of peace about and it showed in their banter back-and-forth.

Mr. Cleary slid his chair back from the table. "I'll be right back. Let me call Matilda and see what she wants." He walked out the kitchen door onto the back porch.

Something worried Cass though. They'd stayed in one place for longer than expected. She wondered if it had something to do with them.

While she continued her dinner, Cass dialed up the sensitivity in her cybernetic ear to listen in on the conversation. The phone rang through to Matilda and her voice sounded over the small speaker clear enough to Cass as if she was standing next to Mr. Cleary.

"Perry, I'm glad you called. Are those two girls still staying with you?"

Mr. Cleary glanced back into the kitchen for a second, then turned back again. "Yeah, why?"

"Because I think there's some trouble associated with them. There were three men here looking for them. They said something about being government agents, but when I pressed them about what agency they were from, I couldn't nail down which one and they wouldn't show me any identification. I guess they figured showing up with a black SUV and pistols on their belts would be enough to scare small-town folks like us."

"So you don't think they're police at all?"

"Not any police I've ever seen. Sometimes, I think city folk think we're all rubes out here in the sticks. If they're federal agents, I'll eat my apron. Be careful. I don't think they're up to anything good. It won't take them long to find someone stupid enough to tell them where those girls went after they left the diner."

"I'll keep that in mind. Thanks for the message, Maddie."

"You don't have to thank me, Perry. I do expect you to come in and have a piece of pie in my diner sometime soon, though."

"I'll take you up on that once we get this all sorted out."

Mr. Cleary cut the phone connection and came back into the kitchen. Cass looked away and pretended to be paying attention to her potatoes. She shot a local wireless message to Shelby's implant as he returned to the table.

"They found us, Shel. We need to go!"

Shelby's eyes met Cass's, as Mr. Cleary said, "I have a question for you, Cass and Shelby. Are you girls in trouble?"

"What kind of trouble do you mean?"

"I got a call from in town that three men were there looking for you two. My friend Maddie didn't think they were up to anything good and called to give us a warning. They're going to find out where you're staying soon enough. Everyone in town knows you're here."

Cass shot a glance at Shelby then said, "I'm sorry, Mr. Cleary. We didn't think this would follow us here and affect you."

"Cass is right. Neither of us wants to bring you or Abby any harm. We'll gather our things and get on the road again right away."

Concern filled Mr. Cleary's eyes. "You're in some kind of trouble, aren't you?"

"It's nothing new you need to worry about," Cass said. "We never would've stayed here if we thought they would find us."

Cass stood up. She and Shelby started to pick up the few personal items they had close by.

Mr. Cleary stood as well and looked at Abby, then back at the two girls who'd gone over to the bench by the door where their backpacks sat.

"Both of you stop right now. You're in some trouble, and I don't kick people off my land when they have something they need from me. Right now, it seems like you need some help."

Shelby shook her head. "These are bad men, Mr. Cleary. They've killed people. We've seen it. They'll not stop at killing you or Abby either if it helps them get what they want. If we're not here and you tell them we've left, they'll probably leave you alone. I'd keep Abby out of sight, though. They don't like cyber humans much."

Mr. Cleary walked over to the back door and closed it. "You two go put your bags in your car, but come back in the house. If you have to leave in a hurry, it'll be better if they're there, so you have them when the time comes. In the meantime let's figure out exactly what we're gonna do when these guys show up. There's no reason anyone has to run from anything while they're on my farm. If it's trouble they want, then trouble is what they'll get."

He stopped and stared at the two girls who just stood and looked at him from across the room. "Go and do as I say. And don't let me catch you sneaking away either. You'll only bring trouble down on yourselves faster. There aren't that many roads out of town. If they know you were here, it won't take them long to catch you. Your only chance is for me to stop them from searching any further for you. I'm going to call Craig Roberts, the Sheriff. He'll send some of his deputies out and we'll find out exactly what kind of federal agents these guys are. We don't take kindly to being pushed around out here."

Cass looked to Shelby. She didn't want to get Abby and her dad in trouble with Sapiens First.

Abby rolled over in her wheelchair to Cass and Shelby. "Do what my daddy says. He won't let anybody hurt you. Neither will I."

"But men are coming with guns," Cass said. "You guys could get hurt."

Shelby nodded. "We don't want you to get hurt, especially after you've been so kind to us."

Abby's eye's turned hard. "Nobody comes on our farm and runs anybody off. They come in for a fight; they'll get one. Do as Daddy says and put your bags in the van. Pull it around back so it's hidden. Park it so you can drive out fast around behind the barn if you need to. Then come back to the house. Daddy and I have some things to do to get ready."

Cass looked from Shelby to Abby and over to Mr. Cleary. He nodded and smiled at them. She realized they needed to rely on somebody to help them right now.

"Alright," Cass said. "Come on, Shel, let's put our stuff in the van and come back in before anybody gets here. Maybe Mr. Cleary can tell them we've left and they'll head on their way."

"You know it won't be that easy, Cass. They're going to want to search the farm, no matter what Mr. Cleary says. Plus, what's going to happen when they find Abby?"

Mr. Cleary asked, "What kind of people are these guys? Why would they have anything to say about Abby?"

"Have you heard of the Sapiens Movement or possibly Sapiens First?"

Mr. Cleary nodded. "I have. That Noble guy is an idiot as far as

I'm concerned. I thought Sapiens First was just a myth, though. You telling me there's some terrorist organization that harms people like Abby?"

Cass and Shelby both nodded.

Shelby said, "We have information that ties them directly to the video of the Saturday Massacre. They've been hunting for us ever since. We've tried to get away time and again, but they keep coming after us." Shelby reached out and squeezed Cass's hand. "We're so tired of running. But we're afraid you're going to get hurt if we stay."

"You let me worry about that." Mr. Cleary pointed to Abby. "Go get the shotguns from the gun safe, and make sure you bring a couple of boxes of shells."

Abby nodded, turned her chair, and rolled away down the hallway to the other side of the house.

Mr. Cleary glanced back at his two guests. "You two know what you need to do. Hurry up. They could be here any minute."

Shelby squeezed past him by the door with Cass right behind her. They left the house and went out to their van, parked by the charging station.

"You know, Shel, we could just leave."

Shelby shook her head. "As much as I worry about them getting hurt, I think we're safer here for now. For whatever reason, they've decided to help us. We have to accept it. Running away at this point is only going to get them in trouble anyway. If we stay, we might be able to help. As you said, once they find Abby, things are going to get worse for them, not better."

Shelby drove the van back around to the back of the farmhouse, parking it behind a large hedge so that it was partially blocked from view. Cass followed and saw the dirt road that circled the rear of the barn. They could get out that way if the attackers somehow blocked the drive on the other side.

Cass took Shelby's hand and headed back toward the farmhouse.

They had no idea what to expect when they got back inside.

What they found was a farmer and his daughter, each armed with pump-action shotguns.

Shelby looked at the guns and Mr. Cleary. "If you meet them like that, they're just going to come out of their car shooting."

"If that's what they want to do, then let them bring it on. We'll deal with them as they deal with us. I've already called the Sheriff. All we have to do is hold them off. He's on the other side of the county dealing with something else. None of his deputies can get here for an hour. Don't worry, though. We'll hold them off that long without a problem."

To punctuate his words, the farmer racked the slide on the shotgun, pumping a shell into the chamber so it was ready to go. "When they get here, you girls stay here in the house. Abby, you stay with them. Be prepared to back me up if it comes to it. Hopefully, I can convince these guys to leave without any violence."

"Sure thing, Daddy. Be careful."

Mr. Cleary smiled. He looked once again at Shelby and Cass and then nodded before he headed out to the farmhouse's wrap-around porch. He sat on a wicker rocking chair there with the shotgun cradled on his lap while he stared out at the sunset over his fields.

Cass was sure someone was going to get hurt. There was no way the Sapiens First team was going to back down in the face of a lone man with a shotgun. They would react with guns of their own, and the shooting would begin. She could only hope it wasn't her friends who were injured once the bullets started flying.

Chapter 18

NO SOONER HAD Mr. Cleary sat down on the porch than Cass picked up the faint whine of an electric vehicle speeding down the farm lane from the main road. Her cybernetic hearing picked it up before anyone else heard it. She ran to the door and called out, "They're here, Mr. Cleary. They're coming down the lane now."

"I see them, Cass. You three stay inside and keep the door closed. If there's trouble, I'll run back to the house, but it's best if I'm facing them from out here for now."

Mr. Cleary stood and moved down to stand at the foot of the porch steps, waiting for the approaching black SUV.

Cass and Shelby followed Abby to one of the front windows in the living room where they could see outside what was happening.

Abby opened the window and propped the barrel of her shotgun on the sill. Her pistol sat in her lap.

The black SUV pulled to a stop about thirty feet away from Mr. Cleary, leaving its headlights on so that they shined on and lit up the house.

Three men got out and stood in a semi-circle facing Mr. Cleary. They all three had guns holstered on their hips. Two of them rested their hands on the weapons but didn't draw them.

"What can I do for you three gentlemen?" Mr. Cleary asked.

"We're federal agents, sir. We're looking for a pair of fugitives who are wanted in relation to an ongoing terrorist investigation."

"Can I see the warrant?"

"Sir, we don't want any kind of trouble. If you know where these two girls are, just tell us and we'll pick them up for you and be on our way."

"I don't know where you come from, but you don't come onto someone's land and start issuing orders. I don't care what kind of agents you are. You know you need a warrant to come here and do anything. I'll ask one more time. Can I see a warrant and some ID please?"

One of the men took a step forward and partially drew a pistol from his holster.

Mr. Cleary swung the barrel of his shotgun around in his direction.

The other man froze but didn't re-holster his pistol.

The farmer kept the shotgun trained on the man holding his gun and said, "I think the three of you should get back in your fancy truck and head back out to the main road. I don't trust you all and you're on private property. I can shoot you for just standing there, since I've asked you to leave. If you want to come talk to me about anything, you come back with the Sheriff. Him, I trust."

The three men all looked at each other. The one in the center shook his head. Then he dodged to the side as he reached for his pistol.

Mr. Cleary fired off a shotgun blast at the one he'd already targeted. It must've struck the man in the leg, because he dropped his pistol and fell down, holding his knee. He howled in pain.

The other two started firing their pistols as Mr. Cleary fired off several more shotgun blasts back at them.

He backpedaled up the steps toward the door as he fired.

The farmer emptied his shotgun, then he fell over sideways, clutching at his midsection.

"Daddy!" Abby exclaimed.

The two men had stopped firing at her father and started forward toward the house.

Without missing a beat, the girl shouldered her shotgun and fired it through the plastic screen in the front window.

Under fire again, the two men raced back for cover behind their truck. They resumed their fire, this time aiming at the house.

Abby didn't duck or move to cover at all. She sat in front of the window in her wheelchair firing until she had no more shells left in her shotgun. Reaching for the box sitting in her lap, she began sliding the cells into the shotgun one at a time. Bullets ripped through the window and walls on either side of her.

Cass and Shelby had ducked behind the sofa.

"Abby, get back from the window," Cass called.

"I'll go get her and pull her back," Shelby said. "You go open the kitchen door and see if you can help her father get inside."

Cass nodded and crawled across the floor into the kitchen.

Shelby ran up behind Abby's wheelchair, grabbed the handles, and pulled her backward.

Abby shouted, "No. Leave me here. They'll kill my father."

"They'll kill all of us if you sit there by that window much longer. Come on. Let's get to the back of the house. Cass is trying to help your father inside. She'll meet us there."

Cass ran for the door. Pulling it open, she crouched down in the darkened doorway and looked for the wounded farmer.

She spotted Mr. Cleary crawling toward the front door. He held the shotgun in one hand as he went. There was a bloody stain on his t-shirt from a bullet wound in his stomach.

Cass propped open the screen door and grabbed his outstretched hand. She pulled with all her might and managed to slide him inside the house.

As soon as he cleared the threshold, she slammed the door closed and locked it. She knew it wouldn't hold them up long, but she had to slow them down somehow.

"Mr. Cleary, can you get up?"

The man had pushed himself to the wall by the door. He sat up so he could prop himself against the wall. He placed his hand over his stomach and then stared at it when it came away covered in blood.

"I am not going to be able to go too much farther right now, Cass. I can hold them here at the door, though."

To punctuate his words, he reached into his pants pocket and started reloading his shotgun.

"Mr. Cleary, you can't stay here. If you let me help you, we can get you to the van. We can take you to the hospital."

"No," Mr. Cleary said, shaking his head. "Look, Cass, you need to do me a favor."

Cass started to argue.

He held up a bloody hand to silence her. "Listen to me, girl. You need to get out of here. You need to go, and you have to take Abby with you. Go. Get out of here. You know if she stays behind, they'll kill her."

"She's not going to want to leave you."

"I don't care. Pick her up and carry her if you have to. Get her out of here. Promise me."

Cass glanced at his belly wound once again and then up at the man's determined eyes. She knew he was right. The Sapiens First team would kill him if they could. If that happened, they'd kill Abby, too.

"Okay, we'll get her out of here. I promise. We'll call for help, too."

"You do that. Now, go! I'll hold them off. Hopefully by the time help gets here, you all will be long gone. Don't come back. Not for anything. If I make it through this, I'll reach out to Abby on her email. Tell her if I don't use the word 'pineapple' in the first sentence, it's not me. Got it?"

"Pineapple. Got it." Cass blinked away tears. "Be careful, Mr. Cleary."

"I'll be as careful as I have to be, girl. Tell Abby I love her."

The tears spilled down her cheeks, and Cass's eyes stung as she backed away from the man sitting by the front door. He struggled up onto his knees so he could peer out the windows on either side of the door. The firing from outside had stopped for now, though she could hear sobbing cries from outside, probably from the man Mr. Cleary shot in that first volley.

Cass ducked low and ran to the back of the house, where Shelby and Abby were waiting by the rear door.

Abby glared at Shelby, then turned to Cass. "Where's my father?"

"He's by the kitchen door. He said he'll hold them off there. He wanted us to take you with us and get out of here."

"I'm not leaving. Give me back my shotgun, Shelby. I need to go help my dad."

Shelby looked at Cass.

Cass shook her head.

The gesture wasn't missed by Abby. "He's hurt, isn't he? Let me go, I need to help him."

"No, Abby," Cass said. "He made me promise not to leave you here. He told me to pick you up and carry you if we have to. I don't want to have to do that, but you need to honor his wishes. Trust me. I'd do anything to have a father like that."

Shelby grimaced and reach down for Abby's hand.

"Here, let me pull you up onto my back piggyback style. We'll run out to the van together."

Cass nodded but then opened up her cerebral implant to the wireless system and the Mantle. She knew it would pinpoint their location for Simon, but she figured that was already a done deal given the response of his attack squad.

She sent out a general 911 call, including a text message regarding armed intruders in a home invasion at the Cleary farm. She put it out on the 911 channel, then added it to the local town message board. She figured some of the local farmers might be interested in knowing someone was attacking their neighbor, too. They might be able to get here before the Sheriff could.

When she was done, she turned to see Shelby hoisting Abby up onto her back. The girl clutched Shelby around her shoulders, holding herself in place.

"Grab the shotgun, Cass. I'm heading out to the van."

"Got it!" Cass said. She picked up the gun. It was heavier than she expected. As she started towards the door, she bent down and grabbed the half-empty box of shotgun shells and Abby's pistol as well. She wasn't sure why, but she figured they might need them if they had to fight their way out past the intruders.

She put everything in the wheelchair and unlocked the wheels so she could push it out to the van. Shelby was still carrying Abby toward the van as Cass caught up.

When they got to the van, Abby said, "Put me in the passenger seat and give me the shotgun. I'll shoot out their tires as we drive by so they can't come after us. Maybe I'll get lucky and get a shot at one of them as well."

Cass nodded and waited until Shelby settled Abby in her seat then handed her the shotgun. She figured she'd owed her a chance at payback against these guys.

The younger girl checked to make sure there was a shell in the chamber, then nodded as she buckled her seatbelt across her chest and waist.

Shelby climbed into the driver's seat.

Cass started to try and wrestle Abby's wheelchair into the van. It was heavy, and she couldn't figure out the mechanism that allowed it to fold up.

A gunshot sounded from the side of the house. It ricocheted off the front of the van.

"They've seen us," Shelby shouted. "Leave the wheelchair. We've got to go."

"But, Abby will need it."

Two more shots rang out.

"No time, Cassie. Get in."

Shelby started the engine and stomped down on the accelerator, pulling out so fast she spit a load of gravel behind her rear tires. They drove around the front of the house.

Abby leaned out the open passenger-side window, firing off shot after shot at the side of the house where the man had come around the corner to fire at them.

Cass dialed in her night vision and saw the man spin away after one of the blasts, clutching at his shoulder.

"Good job, Abby," Cass said. "You got one!"

"Yeah, but I emptied the shotgun to do it. We're not gonna be able the shoot out their tires."

"That's all right," Shelby said. "You said we wanted them to chase after us and leave your father alone, right?"

"Yeah," Abby said with a nod. "I guess you're right."

The van skidded in the gravel around the side of the house and raced past the SUV. The remaining attacker ran out at them with his gun leveled at the van, but he had to dive out-of-the-way at the last instant as Shelby tried to run him down.

As they barreled down the lane towards the main road, Cass looked back in the darkness. All she could see was the headlights of the SUV. Even with her enhanced vision, she couldn't see any of the attackers. They were clear.

"I think we made it, Shel. I don't see them following us."

Abby turned to Shelby. "You too can drop me off in town."

"No," Shelby said. "It's too dangerous. They know you're with us now. They'll only come back for you. You're a witness to what they've done. You have to come west with us, at least until we hear that your dad's okay."

"She's right, Abby. I promised your father we'd keep you safe. This is the only way to make sure for now."

"What good will I be out there away from home?" Abby asked. "I don't have my wheelchair or even my clunky metal legs."

Shelby shook her head. "You don't need them. We'll get you fancy new legs when we get out to San Francisco. There's got to be someplace out there we can get you something that'll fit. You have a universal attachment socket so it'll be a simple fix. We should be able to buy something pretty much off the rack."

For a moment, Abby's eyes sparkled at the thought of having new legs until she realized what that meant she was leaving behind.

"What about my father?"

Cass tried to smile. "He told me to tell you he'd try to email you if everything went well. He told me that you'd know it was really him if he put the word 'pineapple' in the first sentence of the email."

That made Abby laugh out loud. "He knows I hate pineapple." Her laughter turned to a combination of tears and choked off laughs. "He knows that's the best way to make me laugh when I'm sad."

Shelby waited until the van entered the main road, turning off the gravel farm lane. She enabled the auto-drive and turned to Abby. "Your father loves you very much, Abby. I'm sure he'll be alright."

"Plus, I called the Sheriff and the fire department," Cass said. "I also left a message for help on the bulletin board in your community's database."

"Me, too." Shelby reached back to grip Cass's hand. "Great minds think alike, right, Cassie?"

Cass nodded. She leaned forward and placed a hand on Abby's shoulder. "Don't worry, I'm sure he'll be fine. And until we hear from him, you're welcome to stay with us. It'll be an epic road trip."

Abby didn't smile back at Cass. Her face had taken on a somber tone again. She turned to look out the window at the dark skyline and cloudless, starry sky as they raced back up the road toward the highway.

Cass didn't blame her. She knew exactly what it was like leaving behind the only home you knew all your life because of something like this. Cass knew it would take time for Abby to accept the change that had entered her life. She prayed it was only temporary.

Chapter 19

THEY DROVE THROUGH THE NIGHT, letting the van navigate its way west, paralleling the interstate but staying off it. Cass dozed a little but didn't really fall asleep. She kept thinking back to how pale Mr. Cleary had looked when she'd left him sitting there by the door in the farmhouse.

They stopped for a break at a small gas station around midnight. Shelby turned and said, "We can use the restrooms here and get something to eat. I'm hoping by staying to back roads, we'll avoid anyone watching the major rest stops on the interstate. I'll go first. Cass, you stay here with Abby."

Cass nodded and glanced at the younger girl in the front seat. She worried about Abby. Since they left the farm lane, she hadn't said a word.

Cass stared down at her hands. They still had dried blood on them from when she helped Mr. Cleary into the house after he'd been shot. She needed to wash up. Maybe it would help Abby to freshen up some, too.

"Abby, when Shelby comes back, you and I should head into the bathroom and clean up a bit. I think it will help both of us."

"I don't feel like it. Without my wheelchair, I'm a freak."

The statement shocked Cass. It was the first inkling of self-pity she'd heard from the girl since meeting her.

"That's enough of that."

"Enough of what? It's true."

"Then we'll be freaks together. Climb on my back. Here comes Shelby."

Cass got out and pulled open the passenger door. She turned around and looked over her shoulder at Abby. "Come on. I always prefer some company when using a public restroom. I'm not a heathen like Shelby."

"Hey, what was that all about?" Shelby asked as she returned to the van.

Cass smiled and winked at her girlfriend. "Abby and I need some time to clean up a bit. You'll be alright here, won't you?"

"Sure, you ladies go have fun. It's not such a bad restroom as such places go."

Cass laughed. "Abby and I will give our rating when we come back."

Abby grunted something and turned to wrap her arms around Cass's shoulders so Cass could give her a piggy-back ride to the restroom.

Cass smiled as she helped lift the other girl into place on her back. Together they headed around to the side of the rest stop building.

After settling Abby in one of the two stalls, Cass returned to the sink and scrubbed at her hands until they were clean of the blood from the previous night's ordeal. Though she could see they were clean, she still felt like she needed to wash again.

Cass wondered, if she was this traumatized, how must Abby feel? She finished her business and heard the toilet flush in the next stall.

"Abby, you all finished?"

"No, not yet."

"What do you mean? Are you alright?"

"I want to go home. I need to go back and see how my father is.

You two won't let me use my phone to send him a message or anything."

"You know why? We can't afford for anyone to be able to track us down. If you use your phone, there's too much of a chance someone will trace it and find our location. People have to be looking for you, too, by now. Either the authorities, or worse, one of the Sapiens First teams hunting for us."

Abby looked over and glared at Cass. "This is all your fault. If you two had never come to our farm, everything would still be all right."

Cass didn't know what to say. She struggled for an answer. Finally, she settled on the truth.

"You're not wrong, Abby. Shelby and I tried to warn your father that we needed to get back on the road. I think he knew we were running from something. He still opted to let us stay at the farm, knowing that. Now, we are going to pay him back for his kindness by taking care of you."

The door to Abby's stall unlatched. Cass pushed it open to help Abby back up onto her back. The younger girl had been crying, but Cass pretended not to notice. They used some hand sanitizer to wash their hands and headed back out to the van.

Shelby waited by the driver's door. "You want to take a turn behind the wheel for a while? I am bushed. I'm hoping to catch a little sleep in the backseat."

Cass shrugged. "Sure. Let me get Abby settled."

Cass moved over to the passenger side. Abby reached out and pulled herself into the seat and buckled herself in. The girl's arms were strong enough it made lifting herself around like that seem effortless.

Returning to the driver's side, Cass climbed in and started the electric motor.

As Shelby climbed in, she said, "I still don't know how they tracked us down there."

Cass shook her head. "It doesn't make sense. They keep finding us, no matter what we do."

"We just need to keep on the move. They didn't find us right away, so it's likely they have word out about us on their dark bulletin boards or something. I'm sure there are sympathizers around the country who are looking for us on the road. They could be leaving posts saying almost anything about us."

Cass chuckled. "We are criminals of a sort now. Isn't crossing state lines with a minor some sort of crime? They could get us for kidnapping or something?"

Shelby let out a chuckle. "It's probably also a crime leaving the scene of a shooting like we did. We've done that several times now."

"I'll tell them you didn't kidnap me," Abby said, finally engaging with them again. "I would like to know what the plan is for me at this point. You can't keep me with you forever."

Cass looked up into the rearview mirror at Shelby in the back seat.

Shelby shrugged and said, "I don't know in the long term. Look, the plan is to take you with us as far as San Francisco. Once we get Cass's head sorted out, we can find a safe place to drop you off with people we all trust, if that's what you want. They'll be able to check back to see if your father is all right, Abby. They will know how to do it without giving away your location to the wrong people."

"I guess that's alright," Abby said. "I wish there was some way to check in on my father."

"We'll get you a burner tablet the next time we stop. You can start checking your email from time to time. He said he'd check-in."

Cass looked down at the nav map on the dash as the van drove down the state road. "Hey, Shel, how do you have us programmed in for the trip west?"

"I've got us programmed to shadow Interstate-80, but staying on side roads. We should be able to get into Nebraska somewhere near Omaha by midday tomorrow."

"How long will it take us to get to San Francisco sticking to back roads?"

"My guess is it will take us three or four days from here. It's not fast, but I think doing what we're doing will break off the pursuit. They will think we're running as fast as we can. As long as we're careful about staying disconnected from the Mantle, they'll run right past us and not realize we're behind them the whole time."

Abby remained silent for the rest of the night. She fell asleep for a few hours, after they left the service station, for which Cass was glad. Rest would help her out and hopefully settle her mind a little.

They needed to charge up the van again, so they took their time eating while they waited to pick up a larger charge cycle.

If they gave it a good hour hooked up to the fast charging pedestal out front, they'd have enough to get them all the way to Omaha. According to the navigation computer in the van, they should arrive sometime around one or two in the afternoon.

Abby seemed to have retreated into her own thoughts again. She didn't say anything other than what she needed to for her breakfast order.

Cass and Shelby both tried to engage with her to get her to open up and talk, but she just shook her head and looked away. Since she didn't want to talk, the two opted to talk about school and their mutual friends.

It was interesting to Cass that they both talked about school like they'd be going back to the university at some point to finish up. After leaving her home, Cass had assumed school was a lost hope, but when she was with Shelby, the impossible seemed possible somehow.

Shelby always seemed to hold out hope that once they got this all worked out, each of them would have an opportunity to get back to school in some capacity. It would be nice to feel almost normal again.

Their talk lifted Cass's spirits, and she caught Abby smiling a few times when they reminisced about a few of the funnier stories from their first semester at the university. It gave Cass hope that they might be able to pull Abby out of her depression eventually.

They got back on the road with a load of snacks and the promised burner tablet for Abby. She checked her messages right away. From the way her shoulders slumped after checking her email, too, Cass figured there was nothing from her father.

The younger girl turned back to staring out the passenger

window at the passing countryside, while Shelby drove on through the morning.

They arrived in a small town just south of Omaha at two that afternoon. After talking it over, Shelby and Cass decided they could take a chance and checked into a little motel by the old highway.

They left Abby in the van while they both went in to check-in at the motel desk. Behind the counter, an old 2D flatscreen on the wall was tuned to one of the national news networks.

Cass stood behind Shelby, waiting for the clerk to finish up with another customer. Cass looked over at the screen and was shocked when Abby's picture appeared next to the news anchor. The volume was turned down to a murmur but Cass's enhanced hearing tuned in to listen anyway.

"Authorities are still looking for Abigail Cleary, who was abducted from her family home in Indiana sometime yesterday. A nationwide Amber alert has been issued for information related to her disappearance. Little is known about who might have taken her. Her father was found murdered in his home from a gunshot wound late last night after a mysterious 911 call came in to the local dispatch center. We'll have more on this case as updates come in."

Cass turned to see Shelby staring at the same report from in front of the counter.

"You just heard?" Shelby asked.

"Yeah, why don't I go out and make sure our passenger stays put in the van while you finish getting our room set up? I'll wait for you to come out and then we can park near the room together. Maybe you can find something around back with some privacy?"

Shelby nodded and turned her attention back to the clerk, who was just finishing up with the other person.

Cass left the small motel office. Abby sat in the front seat, leaning out the window to watch the few cars that passed by. Cass walked over. "Hey, Abby, why don't you climb in the back seat for a little while? I want to sit up front with Shel."

"I thought we were stopping here to get some rest?"

"We are. I just want to sit up here, that's all. You go back and sit back there for a little bit."

The sixteen-year-old grumbled but climbed out of her seat, directly into the back. Cass climbed in. Shelby wasn't long in coming out. She got in the front of the van and they pulled out of the parking spot to drive around to the motel's rear.

"I got us a room that faces west. That way we can watch the sunset tonight." Shelby looked up in the rearview mirror at Abby. "How are you doing?"

"I'm fine. I just want to go back to sleep."

"You'll have your own bed. I got us a room with two doubles."

Shelby drove around, pulling up in front of room number twenty-four. She handed Cass an old-fashioned plastic key card, then hopped out. Cass got out and opened the sliding door to help Abby out and onto Shelby's back. Cass grabbed the remaining food and their backpacks.

"Let's go inside and get some rest. Then we can figure out what we're going to do next."

"I'm gonna need some clothes, too," Abby said, pointing at Cass and Shelby's backpacks. "I can't wear this stuff for the rest of the trip."

"We'll get you some clothes after we get some sleep," Cass said. "I'm sure there's a Boxmart or something like it with some clothing around here somewhere."

Abby just nodded as Shelby sat her down on the edge of the bed. She hopped off the side of the bed to the carpeted floor, using her hands to sort of walk into the motel room's bathroom.

Cass glanced at Shelby. "Maybe some new clothes will help her feel better."

Shelby smiled. "Shopping always makes me feel better. We'll find someplace to get her something after we all get some sleep. We can do that first thing tomorrow morning before we head out."

"When do we tell her what we just learned from that news report, Shel?"

"Maybe tomorrow. Let's see how things go tonight."

Cass nodded. They couldn't keep Abby's father's death from her forever. Eventually, she'd figure it out. For tonight, though, she could sleep in relative peace.

Hopefully, they all could.

Chapter 20

THE NEXT MORNING, Cass got ready to head out in the van while Shelby stayed back in the room with Abby. She had found a small department store nearby that sold women's clothes.

Abby hadn't taken the news about her father's death well, sinking into a more profound depression, with long periods of sullen silence no matter what Cass and Shelby did to engage with her. They both hoped getting some fresh clothes would help lighten her mood some.

Cass got Abby's sizes from her and grabbed the key to leave.

"I still don't know why I can't come and pick out my own clothes," Abby protested.

Cass said, "It's not safe for you to be out in public. There are reports about you all over the news, so we have to keep you out of sight. You're pretty distinctive given that you're missing your legs and all. People will certainly remember a sixteen-year-old girl missing both legs, especially since we don't have a wheelchair or prosthetic legs for you."

Abby stared down to the stumps at the end of her thighs. Her fists balled up and she shook her head. With a grunt, she rolled over to stare at the wall, away from both Cass and Shelby.

Cass glanced over at Shelby and raised an eyebrow in question.

"It's okay. I've got her. You go get some new clothes and maybe a small backpack or something. I'll wait here."

Cass nodded and went out to the motel parking lot. They'd taken a ground floor room in the back to stay out of sight. Cass still scanned the area for trouble as she walked to the van.

The store was only about ten minutes away. Soon, she was shopping, trying to pick some cute tops to go with the pants she'd found. They'd have to do some alterations on the long pants, but Abby assured them she could make the necessary changes herself if they got her a sewing kit of some kind.

Once Cass had several outfits picked out along with some panties and bras, she headed over to housewares to get the sewing supplies. Along the way, she even found a cute blue canvas backpack in which Abby could keep her stuff. Overall, the shopping trip was a success and Cass headed back to the motel. They had to get back on the road before the checkout deadline at ten.

When she got back to the motel, Shelby and Abby had everything packed and ready to go.

Cass brought in the clothes and backpack so Abby could change into something fresh.

She didn't say anything as she went through the items Cass had selected. She decided on a blue t-shirt featuring a quote from a popular teen holo-drama on the front. She slipped on a pair of gray gym shorts and tucked everything else into the backpack.

"How'd I do?" Cass asked.

"Okay, I guess. I'll work on hemming the pants you bought while we drive."

"Sounds like a plan," Shelby said. "Time to get back on the road." She turned and offered Abby a ride out to the van.

Instead, she slipped the backpack on and hopped down off the bed, walking on her hands out the door and to the van outside.

Shelby shrugged. "Alright, then. Shall we go?"

"The sooner we head out, the sooner we'll find Derek and fix my implant."

They got loaded up in the van with Abby seated in the back seat and started on the road west.

Shelby's estimate of how long it would take them to make it to San Francisco turned out to be accurate. Because they were forced to stay on back roads, the trip all the way to San Francisco ended up taking another two and a half days.

The route took them from Omaha through Salt Lake City and eventually on to San Francisco. They paralleled the interstate almost the whole way, until they got to the Rocky Mountains, where they had to get back on the freeway to cross the pass at the continental divide.

It was late in the afternoon when they drove within sight of the city in the distance. The sun was setting and lit up a beautiful view of the city's skyline.

Shelby looked out the side window at the passing suburbs, as Cass sat behind the wheel while the van drove on in auto-mode.

Cass glanced her way and asked, "What do you think we need to do to find Derek once we get there? I can't access the Mantle, and we've been keeping you off it as well, just in case that was how Simon was tracking us."

"First thing we'll do is find the central community of cyber-humans in the city. There should be some sort of marketplace like the Bizarre back near the university at home. Once we do, we should be able to find somebody who will know how to reach out to someone like Derek. We'll get them to make contact for us."

Cass took her head. "I don't know, Shel. I'm not comfortable letting any more people into our situation. The people we do let in keep getting hurt. First, your parents, then Ramona and Muller, and Abby's dad." Cass glanced over her shoulder. Abby was still asleep in the back seat.

Shelby sighed. "I don't think we have a choice, Cassie. We've got to get some help. Your implant's still screwed up, and that takes precedence. If we can wipe the electronic serial number and get you a new identity, we can start thinking about really disappearing and staying safe forever. Until then, there's really nothing else we can do but keep running."

Cass thought about what Shelby said for a few seconds and gave a half-hearted nod. Shelby was right. They couldn't keep running forever. Once they got to their destination outside of the city, they'd have to start working on finding Derek, and Shelby's plan made the most sense.

She glanced down at the destination computer in the dashboard of the van. They had selected a small motel just to the west of San Francisco in which to stop for the night. They'd be able to get into the city the next day and start looking around.

Cass had been getting steadily weaker day by day. She'd done a good job of hiding it from Shelby and Abby, so far. It was getting hard to keep up appearances, though.

Thankfully, Abby had exerted her independence and insisted on using her hands to get around to and from the van. She no longer let them carry her piggyback, for which Cass was thankful. She definitely wasn't up to it.

They arrived at the destination hotel soon after dinner-time. They stopped at a nearby fast food place to grab some carryout burgers and drinks before they checked in. The check-in process was automated, and Shelby was able to do it remotely from the van without even getting out. She waited until they were on the property and connected locally to the motel, without contacting the larger network or the Mantle.

After they pulled up outside their room, Cass stepped out of the van to stretch her legs. As she did, her legs gave out and she fell to the ground.

"Cassie!" Shelby exclaimed, as she jumped out of the passenger side and ran around to where Cass was sprawled on the ground by the driver's door.

"What happened? Are you all right?"

Cass forced a smile. "I'm fine. Just tripped myself up, getting out."

"That's bull. You're getting weaker, aren't you? You don't think I noticed how you weren't offering to help Abby get around anymore? Even she noticed and mentioned it to me last night."

"I'm fine. Besides, there's nothing we can do until we find

Derek. No sense worrying about it for now."

"Sorry, kiddo. I'm going to worry," Shelby said.

Cass leaned forward and reached up to grab ahold of the seat. With a grunt at the effort, she pulled herself back to her feet, steadying herself for a few seconds before she let go of the van. "Come on, let's go in the room. Then I can lie down and try to get rid of this dizziness."

Shelby reached out to help, but Cass waved her off. "Go help Abby."

"I don't need any help," Abby said. She'd walked herself around the back of the van on her hands after getting out on her own. "You two don't have to keep doing everything for me. I'm used to doing most things on my own. If I need help, I'll ask you for it."

"Fair enough," Shelby said. "Where's your backpack? If you're going to take care of yourself, then carry your own gear."

As Abby frowned and turned around to go back to the other side of the van, Cass shot Shelby a horrified look. "What are you doing?"

Shelby smiled. "If she wants to be treated like a grown-up, then we're gonna treat her like a grown-up. She can remember to carry her own stuff."

Cass wasn't sure that was the right way to handle things with the younger girl, but she was in no position to argue given her current state. She really did need to go lie down.

She reached out to steady herself on the van's hood, as she walked around to the front, and then crossed the small space to the motel room doorway. A few unsteady steps later, she lay on the bed, staring at the ceiling, hoping the weakness and dizziness would pass.

Shelby and Abby carried in the rest of the stuff. Abby was pretty handy, even without legs. Cass should've figured the girl could take care of herself just fine. Perhaps Shelby was right and they'd been coddling her too much.

Cass watched as Shelby carried the last bag of food in from the van. Shelby smiled at her and Cass tried to smile back. Instead, she found herself suddenly overcome with exhaustion. Her eyes drifted closed, her consciousness slipping away.

Chapter 21

CASS WAS unsure how much later it was when she began to awaken again. She heard a familiar voice, though she couldn't place it at first.

"I sure am glad I put the word out to keep an eye open for you two."

Shelby sighed. "Me, too. How did you know we were coming?"

"I got a few notifications over some dark-web channels via Dexter Muller. He and I go way back. He said you gals were looking for me so I put the word out to get back in touch with me if anyone started asking for me around town."

Cass listened in on the conversation, unable to open her eyes right away. She suddenly realized the new voice was that of Derek, the hacker who'd originally helped her hack the cybernetic implant in her head so she could break through the firewall around her home community in the Sapiens Movement enclave.

She tried to say something, to let them know she could hear them, but found herself unable to speak. She couldn't open her eyes either.

What was happening to her?

Panic struck at Cass, making her wonder if there had been some sort of failure in her implant. She could be paralyzed now.

Cass struggled to move any muscle anywhere in her body.

She must've succeeded somewhere, because Shelby said, "Did you see her hand? It moved. Her finger twitched, I saw it."

"She must be coming around. The new firmware install is almost done. It's probably re-booting some of the systems which shut down as she slipped into the coma."

"Will there be any permanent damage?"

"I can't tell from what I've seen in the system so far. I can't be sure, but everything seemed to be software-related. Once I was able to remove the broken *Protocol One* folder and repair the damage to the underlying firmware, I think her whole system, including her brain's neural connections, will all reset on their own."

As if to support Derek's words, Cass felt more of her muscles begin to answer to her repeated commands to move. Her eyes fluttered open and her mouth began to move as she tried to form words. "What – What happened? All I remember is falling asleep."

Shelby's face leaned over the bed where Cass lay staring at the ceiling.

"Cassie, honey, we haven't been able to wake you up for over a day. I finally went into the city out of pure desperation to try and find Derek. I thought I'd failed, but when I returned here, I found him waiting outside the room for me. Abby wouldn't let him in."

The thought of the legless girl keeping the short-statured Derek out of the room brought a tired half-smile to Cass's face. The image it conjured in her mind amused her.

Cass found she could turn her head now. She shifted to the right, spotting Derek, standing next to Shelby and Abby, seated on the other bed behind them.

"I was out for over a day?"

Derek nodded. "Your entire system, cyber and organic, started to shut down. Subroutines that had been overwritten by the corrupted *Protocol One* file started to crash. I'm glad I got here when I did. I'm afraid to think of what would happen if I'd been too much longer. It appears as if your entire implant was about to melt down from a software standpoint."

"It was bad, Cass," Shelby said. "He had to reinstall everything from scratch, which meant wiping the implant clean, to the point you stopped breathing for a few seconds."

"Lucky for you," Derek said. "I always pull backups of any systems I upgrade. I had the original firmware subset I pulled from your implant before I installed the original *Protocol One* file. I was able to re-initialize that in your system with an emergency reset to keep you alive. Then it rebuilt the original subroutines on its own. That's why you're having trouble getting some of your muscle control and other things back. Give it some time, it'll all return, probably in the next hour or so."

Cass tried to sit up but found herself unable to muster the strength or muscle command to accomplish it.

"Any sign of people following us, Shel?" Cass asked.

"No. So far, so good."

Derek smiled. "I think you're in the clear now. My guess is they were tracking her via a hidden subroutine that their enclave IT administrator jacked into the *Protocol One* system when the firewall defenses overwhelmed your implant originally. That's how they've been tracking you. When certain functions occurred within your implant, the system opened up a secret channel to the Mantle and checked in. Luckily, you guys have been on the run and staying up and awake for long periods, which I think was what confounded that part of the system. You were always just far enough away that they couldn't quite catch up."

Cass looked from Derek to Shelby and back again, "So, that means we're in the clear? They can't find me anymore?"

Derek nodded. "I wiped the system ID from your implant with the new firmware install. There's no way to identify you any more using that part of your implant. Of course, there's still standard facial recognition on open public surveillance cameras and things like that. Incidentally, there's quite a search going on for your young friend over there," Derek said, hooking a thumb over his shoulder at Abby.

"We had to bring her with us. There was no way to leave her there safely. We're hoping now that things are settled with my implant, we can find a way to return her back to her family."

"Abby," Shelby asked. "Do you have any family back in Indiana we can contact?"

The question it brought tears to Abby's eyes. She shook her head. "Dad and I have been alone since Mom died. I think some of her family live somewhere up north, but she didn't talk to them much and I never met them."

Shelby shook her head. "I honestly don't know what to do, Derek. She's pretty much an orphan. I'm afraid if we hand her over to any local authorities, she might be in danger from Sapiens First teams coming to look for her. She's a witness to the people who shot her father. Is there someplace we can find that is safe for her here in San Francisco?"

Derek scratched his head as he stared at the ceiling. "There might be someplace, but we need to do something about the way she looks. Her face has been all over the news and everyone knows she's missing both her legs. Anyone seeing a girl without prosthetics is going to be pretty suspicious anyway. Given her age and her appearance, it won't take much for anyone to put two and two together."

Cass, able to move a little more now, shifted her body to one side and lifted herself up on one elbow so she could see better. "We have a little of the money Ramona sent us left. What do you think, Shel? Will that be enough to cover a new pair of legs for her?"

Shelby shrugged. "I'm not sure. My arm was more than the cost of what we have left, and we have to get two legs for her."

"I think I can help you with that a little," Derek said. "There is a community outreach foundation here in San Francisco that offers open-source funding for individuals without the financial where-withal to cover expenses for necessary cybernetic prosthetics. We could also get her an old plastic leg, without any electronics at all, for nothing from nearly any hospital, though it would probably risk having her identified once the medical bots got her into the system.

The foundation is the best bet. I know somebody on the inside who can help us. And, they won't ask too many questions."

Shelby nodded. "Do that, then. I think it's time Abby got some real legs for a change." She turned to Abby. "I know you were attached to the ones your father built for you back on the farm. Do you think you'd like a pair of legs with some slick skin, like my arm?"

Abby frowned and her brow creased for a moment as if she was getting ready to argue, but then she seemed to change her mind.

She gave a sort of half-smile and said, "I guess I can at least take a look at what's available."

Shelby smiled and nodded. "I'll take it. That's good enough for me. We'll follow up with Derek as soon as Cass can get up and move around on her own."

Cass realized there was another thing weighing on her mind now that her implant was taken care of. She wondered how much time they had before trouble caught up with them again in some other way. Derek was right about how there were other ways to track them down. She didn't relish the idea of living on the run forever.

"Derek," Cass said. "Do you know about the video we shot?"

Derek nodded. "You both know you're going to have to do something to get them off your back. They aren't going to stop coming after you. They have to discredit the video once and for all. I've seen public outcry welling up as the video gains more traction."

"That's what I was afraid of. I know Simon Cantwell isn't the type to give up just because one way of tracking me has gone away. He's relentless."

"Yeah," Shelby asked, "but how do we fix it?"

Derek said, "The only way to fix this for good is for you both to come out in the open and make it all public."

The answer shocked Cass. She'd thought that they were just going to keep it to themselves and they'd be able to live out the rest of their lives happily ever after. Now, Derek's revelation had thrown a bucket of cold water all over her happy little fantasy.

Cass shrugged. "I don't know what we could do to convince

anyone of anything. All we have is the video. People have already seen it and have their opinions."

Derek thought for a moment before responding. "There is a reporter I know who covers tech stories here for the Chronicle. I think perhaps I could reach out to her. Honestly, this would be the scoop of the century for any reporter. It would bring down a high-pitched visibility political figure, expose a hidden terrorist organization, and discredit an entire political movement. It would be huge."

"I don't care about any of that," Shelby said. "Neither does Cass. We just want to be left alone."

"I understand that. I think this reporter is the way to do that. Believe me. The last thing I want anyone to do is to become more visible. In your case, though, you've got to go public before you can get your life back. The reporter will be able to verify and validate everything that happened, once they have access to the original recordings. That, coupled with your testimony about who and what was really behind the Saturday Massacre, should be enough for her to put the rest of the puzzle pieces together. A good investigative reporter should be able to connect the rest of the dots. Other news outlets will take the story and expose everything else as the whole operations falls apart. Do you want me to reach out to her?"

Derek looked from Cass to Shelby, waiting for an answer.

Shelby glanced at Cass.

Cass smiled back at her. It wasn't like they really had any choice. "Do it."

Shelby nodded in return. "She's right. Do it. Set up a meeting and we'll sit down with this reporter friend."

Cass relaxed to lay back on the bed again. Her muscles still weren't entirely in her command, and it had been a struggle to stay up on her side like that.

The good news was, she could feel more control returning as the implant's neuromuscular interfaces reinstalled themselves. It was a pain in the neck to have to wait.

"Shel, hon, I'm going to rest some more. I'm feeling lots better but I'm still super tired."

"Go to sleep, sweetie. Now that I know you'll wake up again, it's fine."

Cass closed her eyes. Before falling asleep, she set a wake-up alert in the implant's system to let her know once all of the new installations were complete.

With that finished, Cass drifted off again. There'd be more to do soon and she needed more rest.

Chapter 22

CASS AND SHELBY had to wait until the next day before Derek got back to them.

Both their systems chimed at the same time with a message.

The message was from Derek.

The reporter is ready to talk. Her name is Meredith Langston. She has arranged to meet you at a café downtown. She figured you'd appreciate a public place where you could feel safe.

Let me know if you agree to the meeting and I'll tell her the time. I've attached a recent publicity picture of her so you'll recognize her when you see her.

Also, I got the OK to bring Abby in for those legs we talked about. The contact I have was very sympathetic when I explained the delicate nature of the situation. He agreed that she needed legs sooner rather than later.

You can bring her in this afternoon on your way to the meet up at the café. I'll keep an eye on her while you're with Meredith. When you get back, she should have the new installations in place.

Derek

Shelby looked her way almost immediately. "Did you get the message?"

Cass nodded. "Looks like good news all the way around, doesn't it?"

Shelby nodded and looked around. "Where's Abby?"

"She's out by the van, sitting on one of the folding chairs Ramona had stashed in the back. She said she needed some sun."

Shelby got up, heading to the door. She was about to open it when shouting came from outside.

It was Abby. "Cass! Shelby! Help, they're here!

Shelby yanked the door open.

They both raced outside to see two men dressed in black grappling with Abby. She struggled and tried to punch at them while they grappled with her. It almost would have been amusing if it weren't for the fact that Cass knew exactly who those men represented. She was about to run to Abby's defense when more black-clad individuals appeared, both men and women.

Before they could do anything, Cass and Shelby were blindsided and tackled to the ground. Out of the corner of Cass's eye, she could see that they had Abby as well.

A familiar voice came back from behind her. It sent a chill down Cass's spine.

Simon Cantwell stepped into view above Cass. He leered down at her. "Put them in the back of their own van. Then follow us out of here."

He pointed to some more of his thugs. "Stay here and get rid of all evidence that they were here."

The Sapiens First leader looked back down at Cass and Shelby. "You two have been quite hard to find. I almost could have enjoyed the chase if it weren't for the fact that you've caused a lot of trouble, along with the deaths of quite a few of my best people."

"Too bad a bullet didn't find you, too," Cass sneered. It wasn't much of an act of defiance, but it was all she could do given the circumstances. Deep inside, though, she felt a deep sense of despair. There didn't seem to be anything anyone could do to get them out of this predicament.

"Get them out of sight. We need to get back to the temporary base, then we can do some proper questioning." Simon turned to leave and the people gripping Cass and Shelby followed his instructions.

Their hands and legs were tied together with zip-ties, the tight plastic cutting into Cass's wrist and ankles. Someone pulled a black cloth bag with a silvery interior over her head.

As soon as the bag was pulled into place, Cass felt all connection to the web and Mantle cut off. The hoods were shielded somehow, keeping both Cass and Shelby from contacting anyone to help them.

The Sapiens First team tossed all three of their captives on top of each other in the back of Ramona's white van. Cass heard several voices calling out instructions to load up, as the van's electric motor began to hum.

With a lurch, the van pulled out of the parking place and sped away from the motel, headed for someplace Cass was sure they would have a tough time escaping.

They drove for almost an hour and Cass gave up trying to come up with a way to remember parts of their route. With her eyes covered and her implant blocked, she couldn't make any sense of the sounds that filtered into the back of the van.

The van finally stopped and voices from outside shouted something about driving inside. The vehicle moved forward for a few seconds and then stopped for the final time.

The rear doors opened. Hands grabbed at Cass, hauling her from the back of the van onto her feet. She stood still as someone came over and yanked the bag from her head.

Cass blinked at the bright sunlight spilling in through the skylight overhead. They stood beside Ramona's van in a large, empty warehouse. She instantly tried to reach out with her implant and found no signal to which she could connect. The building had been shielded to prevent outside connections, even with the glass windows and skylight above.

Against one wall was a staircase up to a small loft above the open warehouse floor below. There were six doors along that upper walkway.

Cass's attention turned to those holding them as Simon Cantwell walked over to them from a line of black SUVs parked near their van.

Simon pointed at Shelby. "Disable the Moore girl's implant. I don't want her trying anything with that arm of hers."

A man standing nearby nodded. He had a baton attached to his belt that Cass remembered all too well. He approached Shelby, who was held on both sides by two other black-clad Sapiens First goons.

The man lifted the foot-long baton from his belt and reached up until he tapped the end on Shelby's implant.

She spasmed but was held up until she regained her feet. Her left arm hung limp at her side, useless now that the cerebral implant's interface had been shut down. Shelby's V-tats had all gone blank, too, leaving patches of her skin looking like they had a milky film stretched over it.

The guy with the baton pointed at Abby. "What about the younger one. Should I shut down the sockets on her legs?"

Simon laughed. "She doesn't have any legs to put into them. I don't think she's any danger to anyone. Besides, she doesn't appear to have a cerebral implant, so she's not contacting anyone."

The guy nodded and returned to his spot, standing in line with the others who weren't holding the prisoners.

Simon pointed at Cass and gestured toward the stairs. "Bring her with me to the office. The other two can be locked up. Wherever it is, Carter, make sure the door is secure. We can't risk them getting away and calling for help."

One of the group, who Cass assumed was Carter, stepped forward. "Got it, boss. There's a room already set up. We even have video surveillance in there to keep an eye on them."

Simon nodded. "Good work. Bring the Armstrong girl along. We have some talking to do."

Cass looked back at Shelby as they pulled her toward the stairs. Her mind raced through what she saw in the warehouse around them, trying to come up with some way out. She didn't see anything that could help them. Cass didn't know how they could possibly get out of this.

Shelby gave Cass half a smile as if to try and reassure her, but Cass could tell her heart wasn't in it. This wasn't good. They both knew it.

Of the three, Abby seemed the most defiant, though she had the least she could probably do, given the fact she didn't have legs.

They followed Simon up the steps to the first door along the catwalk, by the stairs. The others were brought up the steps behind her.

The two guards escorting her shoved her into the office, following her and Simon inside, shutting the door. The others, led by the one called Carter, must be headed for one of the other rooms farther down the catwalk.

One of the men turned Cass around to face the wall and cut the zip-tie around her wrists, freeing her hands. He spun her back around and pushed her toward a desk and chair along the far wall. Cass took the hint and sat down, rubbing at the welts on her wrists from the plastic bindings.

The two men walked over to stand by the only exit.

Simon sat down behind the metal desk nearest Cass. He tapped a few things on an open laptop sitting there, then made a few adjustments on a small tripod, topped by a webcam attached to the computer with a long black wire.

"Cass, we're going to have a discussion, you and I. As I've told you in the past, when we had our last conversation, I am not going to tolerate any lying or deception. You already know I can get out of you whatever it is I want. That takes time and effort I don't have time for. I would like to retrieve the information I need sooner rather than later."

"I don't know what you think I can provide you, Simon. Did you think I was just going to give some sort of a confession or something? If that's what you want, it's hardly the truth. I know what I saw. I know the video is real."

Simon nodded. "That's exactly what you're going to do, Cass. You're going to answer all my questions and then you're going to look into this camera and recant the accuracy of the video, telling the whole world how you made the whole thing up so you could get back at your parents for threatening to pull you out of school."

"But my parents didn't threaten to do that until after the video had been recorded."

"Ah, but it's important to have a kernel of truth at the center of this video. That kernel of truth will bolster the effectiveness of your confession about how you made it all up, in collusion with radical subs just like yourself."

Simon smiled as he continued. "People won't find it hard to believe an entitled, spoiled rich girl sought revenge against her father and his beliefs after everything was taken from her."

Cass realized what he said was true. She needed to try to hold out. She had to show some sort of active defiance in the face of Simon's confidence.

At first, she wasn't sure what she could do until she realized the beginning of a plan. It wouldn't help her or her friends get away, but it might give them some leverage down the road if they ever did escape from Simon's clutches.

Cass was thankful they hadn't shut down her implant like they had Shelby's. They still needed what Cass was holding in her memory bank.

She switched on her video recording function via her ocular and auditory implants. Now everything Simon said to her would be recorded.

Simon adjusted the camera on the tripod again while watching the image on the laptop's screen until he was satisfied with the framing.

He looked at Cass with that same cold-hearted grin that never quite showed in his eyes. "Now, Cass, we are going to have a question-and-answer session. As you remember, I can force you to say anything I want. I'd rather not have to resort to those measures."

Cass forced a smile of her own. "I suppose it wouldn't look good for your video to record you torturing me the way you did back at my parents' house in the enclave, would it?"

"Video can be edited. I can show the necessary things I need to show without giving them the whole video. People are so gullible, they'll believe anything they see or hear."

Cass scrambled for something else to say. She had to delay him and keep him talking. "You're not going to hurt me, at least not permanently. You can't afford to."

"What makes you say that?"

"I know that because you have to return me to my father. He's too highly placed in the Movement and I don't think you want him complaining about your methods to Sterling Noble."

Cass wasn't sure her ploy would work. Her dad had already given her over to torture once. She was pretty sure he'd written her off at this point, but Simon didn't need to know she thought that.

Simon dashed her hopes as he said, "My dear, your father and mother are under investigation for the circumstances surrounding your escape. They have no power to influence anything anymore, I assure you. No one believes you overpowered two of my best men all by yourself. Neither of them can tell me what happened for sure, since one is dead and the other may never wake up, but rest assured, I will get to the bottom of the matter. You will help with that as well."

That answer shocked Cass. When her mother helped her escape, they'd done everything they could to make sure all signs pointed to Cass working on her own. If Simon forced her to testify about that as well, Cass wasn't sure she could resist giving up the role her mother had played in the escape.

Simon continued, "Mr. Noble and I have had many discussions about the influence the vaunted James Armstrong has in the Movement. We've decided that an example needs to be made of him and your mother. I think we might even bring your sister in on it. People need to know what happens when someone betrays the Movement."

"My sister had nothing to do with it," Cass blurted out without thinking.

Simon smiled and pointed at the camera. "Go on. It looks like you're trying to tell me something. You were saying—"

Cass bit at her lip in frustration. Dammit, she hadn't meant to lose control like that. She should be happy that her sister, who'd betrayed her to everyone, was implicated in her escape. As angry she was at Elena, though, she couldn't let her get caught up with Simon and his thugs. Who knew what Simon might have meant when he said he'd make an example of them?

Cass changed the subject. "So you and Mr. Noble Talk often? I figured that must be the case. He's long denied the existence of Sapiens First, but he had to be in direct charge of your operation all along. That was the only way your organization could exist and get funding."

Simon nodded. "Very astute of you. Actually, Sapiens First was Mr. Noble's idea from the very beginning. He knew we would need a segment of our Movement's membership who would be willing to do the things that needed to be done when purely political means failed to achieve what we needed. That's why he recruited me to come in and assemble those individuals into an organization of true believers."

Cass suppressed a smile. She pressed on. "But you're not a true believer, are you? You're something worse, a person who does the horrible things you do for money. Or do you do it just because you enjoy causing pain?"

Simon laughed. "Are you kidding? I love technology. I have the best technology I can around me at all times. That's how I keep up with people like you, without submitting to the butchery."

"What about them?" Cass said, pointing to the men by the door. "Won't they be a little shocked to hear you talk about technology that way?"

One of the men at the door chuckled a little but didn't say anything. The other one shook his head and went back to checking something under one of his fingernails.

Simon smiled. "I'm smart enough to surround myself with people who know how to get the job done any way it needs to get done. I can't afford to be limited by those who are reluctant to handle certain technologies because of fear or distrust. This particular group is among the best of my hand-picked followers. They do what they're told to do because they get paid a lot to do it."

"So, Sapiens First has no people you consider true believers?"

"Oh, there are many so-called true believers who do random acts of violence for us across the country. There are even those who would kill if I asked them to. That, however, is something I try to avoid. People like that make mistakes and are untrustworthy. Because of that, none of them know exactly who I am or even how to contact me directly. I always reach out to them through secure channels. It's important for me to keep them separated from each other. In fact, the only place all of their names are located is on this laptop."

Cass tried to think of something else to ask him. All she could focus on was how Simon's whole operation was nothing like she expected. They were just mercenaries. They were doing illegal and horrible things simply because someone paid them to do it. Somehow, that disgusted her even more than what she'd thought of them before.

Simon stood up. "Enough of this idle chatter. You, my dear Cass, are going to tell me what I need to know about your escape. Then, we'll create a new recording where you confess to working with your girlfriend to fake the Saturday Massacre video. You're going to tell people how sorry you are at the trouble it's caused, just because you were angry with your parents. Finally, you're going to tell them you have given me all the original video files so I could verify how you pulled off such convincing alterations."

Cass shook her head. "What good is that going to do you? If you have all the footage, it'll only show that the confession was coerced. It'll show the events happened exactly as I released them the first time. Besides, you know the authorities are going to want to question me themselves. Your lie will never hold up."

Simon sighed. "Unfortunately, my dear, you will have an unfortunate accident and will not be around to share those videos files with anyone else. During your attempt to escape my perfectly legal custody, en route to delivering you to the Federal authorities, you will have a fatal accident that will permanently disable your implant beyond the point of data recovery."

Cass gasped as she finally had confirmation of what awaited her if she didn't escape.

Simon offered a sad grin at her reaction. "Yes, you and your two friends will be found days from now, dumped in some landfill. We will make it look like you were all rescued from my custody, only to be later killed by a group of sub-human thugs who wanted to stop you from confessing."

Simon chuckled before he continued, "It's really quite ingenious. I expose the video as a fake, get the public all riled up about the subs who have killed your young friend, Abby, who of course is innocent in all of this. She will make a nice rallying cry for what happens when sub-humans are left unmonitored. And at the end of it all, Sterling Noble will have a huge boost in the political polls just before an important election."

Cass wasn't even shocked. It didn't surprise her. She already knew he was capable of murder for political gain. Even if she couldn't escape, she had to keep recording everything on the outside chance that maybe somebody would recover that video and see it after her death. It was the only thing she could think of doing, given her chances for escape were slim.

Playing along, trying to let Simon think he'd defeated her, Cass let her shoulders sag and head slump forward. As she did, Cass saw the row of video monitors on one wall, all plugged into a computer system on a nearby desk. On one of the screens, Cass saw Shelby and Abby seated on the floor of an empty room.

A wild thought occurred to Cass. It was the sort of idea born of desperation, where the brain brought together random facts and memories in strange ways. Her idea spurred the barest inkling of a plan, a crazy plan only she could put into action.

Simon distracted her from her thoughts. "I'll tell you what, Cass. If you tell me everything I need to know, say everything I need to say on the first go around, without me having to prompt you, I'll make your death and the death of your friends quick. I promise.

None of you will feel any pain. Your deaths are inevitable, but that is something I can offer you."

Cass resisted the urge to lift her head and glare at him. Instead, she stared at the floor between her knees, where she sat and shook her head, while she continued to work on her plan. "You don't have to kill Abby. She doesn't know anything about this. If you let her go, she'll be unable to say anything about what's going on."

"Unfortunately, she suits our needs a little too well for me to let her go. People need to see the death of an innocent child for political gain by the twisted minds of those corrupted by the Mantle."

Cass sighed, hoping he didn't see through her deception. "Very well. I'll tell you what you want, but I expect you to keep your promise."

"I have no reason to lie to you, Cass. It makes no difference to me how I achieve my goals. I'll keep my promise if you hold up your end of the bargain. Now, shall we get started? I still have to put this all together and make sure everything is set up for release. You and your friends will have one last night together. Then, once I have assembled the evidence in the way I need it, I will complete my end of our little bargain."

Cass ground her teeth together; her mind whirling through possibilities. She was only going to get one shot at this.

Lifting her head, Cass stared directly into the webcam, directing an invisible laser from her ocular implant into the center of the lens. She had to concentrate while at the same time listening to the questions coming from Simon.

He asked his questions and Cass went along with everything he prompted her to say, answering in a monotone, almost as if she wasn't entirely there.

Chapter 23

CASS STRUGGLED to focus as the guards took her from the office. They walked her down the catwalk to the final door along the row. Mental exhaustion threatened to overwhelm her as one of the guards shoved her into a small square room before locking the door behind her.

Shelby caught Cass with one arm and pulled her into an embrace. Her left arm, the cybernetic one, hung limp at her side. Abby sat on the floor, leaning up against the wall nearby.

"You were gone a long time, Cass. Abby and I were afraid you weren't coming back at all. What did they do to you?"

Cass glanced up at the camera in the corner of the room, the tiny red light indicating it was on and recording the room's occupants. She paused to make sure she didn't say anything that might give away the details of her plan. "They wanted me to give up and tell them the recording was all faked. Then Simon jacked into my implant and downloaded all of the files from the rally."

Shelby took a step back. "No. Cass, you didn't do what he wanted, did you?"

When Cass didn't answer right away, Shelby couldn't hide her shock. "Cass, why?"

"Because there was nothing else I could do. I've been questioned by Simon before. You know that. He was going to get what he wanted out of me. Nothing was going to stop him. The same is true for him getting the files. It wasn't like I could keep him from plugging into my implant. This way, I felt like I at least controlled some of the situation."

"Cass, that's crazy. Now that he has everything he needs, he has no reason to keep us alive."

Cass couldn't let out her plan. Not yet. Besides, it was only partially complete.

"I had to trade the only thing I had."

"Cassie, what did you trade?"

"I traded my resistance for peace. Simon told me the end would be painless. That was the only option I had."

"End?" Abby asked. "Do you mean they're going to kill us? We have to do something. We have to find a way out of here."

Shelby paced across the room and back again. Even with one arm disabled to swing limp at her side, she looked like a caged tiger pondering what she'd do on the day the keepers removed the bars.

Cass shook her head. "Shelby, I didn't give up. I made the best of a bad situation. And it's not over yet."

When Shelby turned to say something and met Cass's eyes, Cass nodded up toward the camera in the corner.

Shelby followed her gaze and then looked back at Cass, this time with the hint of a smile on her face. She crossed over to pull Cass into another one-armed embrace.

Shelby leaned in and whispered, "I hope you have a plan."

"I do," Cass said in her quietest voice so only Shelby could hear. "Give me a boost up into the corner so I can look at that camera more closely."

Shelby released her embrace, glancing at the camera then back at Cass, an unanswered question in her eyes.

"Trust me, Shel."

Shelby nodded and went over to the corner with Cass. She bent down with her one hand extended to try and lift Cass up, while she balanced herself using the wall.

"What are you doing?" Abby asked from the other side of the room. She got up on her hands and walked over to where the two worked on getting Cass lifted up closer to the camera. It wasn't working with Shelby only having one working arm.

Abby tapped on Cass's leg. "Let me help. You can stand on my shoulders."

Cass grimaced. "I can't do that."

"Sure you can. I'm tough, and my younger cousins do it all the time when they come over. We call it our circus clown act. My shoulders are tough, and I'm pretty strong. I'll sit there in the corner. Shelby can help you get up on my shoulders. That should make you tall enough to see what you need to see."

Shelby nodded as Abby moved into the corner and turned around, facing outward. She looked up at Cass and smiled. "Step right up. If we're going to get out of here, I figure it's going to take all three of us. Just because I don't have legs, doesn't mean there is no way for me to help."

Cass reached out to Shelby to steady herself on her girlfriend's shoulder. She placed one foot on Abby's left shoulder, then stepped up with Shelby's help until her other foot rested on the opposite shoulder.

Looking up, Cass was just high enough to see what she needed to see. She stared into the camera lens, activating the laser input she'd discovered during the Federal Reserve job.

Letting herself and her awareness of her surroundings go, Cass tried to focus in on the image coming in via her implant. The connection through the lens reached the internal electronics, and Cass found the link back to the computers running the building's security camera systems.

Cass reached out and felt herself pulled into the data stream. She surfed down the stream until she reached the familiar landscape of the internal computer circuitry with its busy pathways between the various circuits.

Now, she had to get to work.

The experience upon entering the stream of circuits and connections was much different this time for Cass, compared to the time she'd entered the node at the Federal Reserve in Pittsburgh. This time, she felt in control.

From the circuit she was in now, Cass could see feeds coming in from other cameras as well as other links to connected devices. The first thing she did was find a piece of video from their room's camera and looped it so none of the guards would see anything unusual. It would also stop active recording in their cell, so they could talk through Cass's plans when she returned to her body.

Once that was done, Cass looked for a way out of the closed security camera network. She followed the flow of signals around her until she spotted one of them that caught her attention. She followed the linkage down the line until she reached a more complex layout of circuitry.

From there, Cass looked for a way out. She knew there had to be a link from this system that led outside the building's shielded exterior.

She scanned the traffic all around her, looking for something that might be a signal leading out. She spotted one that looked familiar and followed it.

Cass smiled as the speeding electronic signal reached the building's central communications router. There was a connection that seemed brighter than the others, somehow both more substantial, and more colorful. That had to be their connection to the outside.

She moved to the connection point but found herself held back by something. It felt like she was pressing against a flexible barrier, like pushing at a giant rubber membrane. Something kept her from getting through to the other side. It took her a moment before she realized that the person who set up this network had installed some sort of a firewall.

The firewall seemed to be permeable in some ways, though. She saw some signals passing through in both directions. Cass pressed in certain places where information seemed to be traveling through the membrane. She could sort of force a finger or two through along with the incoming and outgoing traffic but reached a point where she got stuck.

Cass realized she was going about this the wrong way. She was thinking in terms of her physical self, which was limiting her ability to travel through the network. Refocusing back on how she felt when she first got drawn into the connection, she visualized sand flowing through the narrow gap in an hourglass.

It worked.

Grasping at a passing signal, it pulled her along one of the outgoing streams until she was suddenly outside the building. She had a direct connection to the Mantle again as information flooded into her mind.

Cass started to reach out and found she was limited in what she could do and the information she could send. She was not jacked into the Mantle in the usual sense.

Knowing she couldn't take too long doing this, she looked around from inside the thin data stream she'd attached to. Cass tried to determine their exact location, eventually settling on copying an IP address that seemed to be assigned to this particular building node.

Unsure how she could use this information, Cass thought about who she could send it to. There was only one person she knew in the San Francisco area, so she added an identifier tag for Derek and sent the text of the building IP address out to him.

As soon as she did so, a tugging at her consciousness yanked her backward. She snapped back like a slingshot pulling her in reverse. A few seconds later, Cass gasped as her consciousness returned to her body.

She fell backward, her arms flailing as Shelby struggled to catch her when she toppled from Abby's shoulders. In the end, it sort of became a controlled fall to the floor.

Cass looked up at Shelby. "Wow, that was intense."

"Cassie, what did you—?" Shelby asked, then stopped herself as she glanced back at the camera.

"It's okay, Shel. We can talk freely now."

"Good, now, what did you just do?"

"I sort of went into the system the same way I did at the Federal Reserve node. I wasn't sure if I could do it or not, but I tried it when Simon questioned me. I was able to access his computer via the camera he used to record me. I downloaded all his files. I know everything about the Sapiens First arm of the movement. Names, places, dates, everything."

"What about now, Cass? Did you get help for us?"

Cass shrugged. "I got outside, sort of. I was able to send a short message. I'm just not sure if anyone will get it or if they'll even understand what it is."

Abby moved over to the other two. "Who did you send a message to?"

"I couldn't think of anyone else we knew in the area, so I just tagged Derek in the message and attached a copy of the warehouse's IP address. Hopefully, he'll understand what it is and be able to tell it was from me."

"How will he know?" Shelby asked.

"Not sure," Cass said. "I'll try again a little later. I'm feeling really tired all the sudden."

"Maybe we can try in the morning," Abby said.

"We'll see," Cass said. She didn't want to tell Abby that she was pretty sure Simon was coming to begin covering his tracks in the morning, which meant the end for all three of them. She had to let the girl cling to the hope that Derek would get the message and send help.

Chapter 24

CASS WOKE up when she heard someone say her name.

"You awake, Cass?" Abby asked.

"Sure. What's up?" Cass sat up and rubbed her eyes.

"The camera has been acting weird for the last fifteen or twenty minutes."

Cass turned to look at the camera in the corner.

Apparently, Shelby couldn't sleep either. She asked, "What's weird about it?"

"Well, the light used to be solid red all the time which I guess meant it was turned on or recording. For the last twenty minutes, though, it's been blinking kind of erratically on and off. I don't know if the connection is bad, or if the power's going out in the building, or what."

Cass stared at the camera to try and see what the younger girl saw. Sure enough, the light was blinking, and not in a regular pattern. It was flashing on and off in erratic bursts of long and short flashes.

"That's so weird. What do you think, Shelby? It's almost as if it's sending some sort of…"

Together the both of them said, "Code."

Cass turned her head to stare at Shelby, then got up and walked across the room with Shelby right behind her as they stared up at the camera.

"I wonder if maybe someone's trying to tell us something?" Cass asked. She turned to Shelby. "Do you know anything like Morse code or anything like that?"

Shelby shook her head.

From across the room, Abby said, "It's not Morse code. I already tried that. I learned it in Girl Scouts. It doesn't match up with anything I learned there when we covered radio communications."

Cass turned to Abby. "But you think it's a code, too, right?"

Abby nodded. "I think so, but it's not one I know. That's why I thought it was maybe just broken."

"I don't think so, kid," Shelby said. "If someone is trying to get a hold of us, we've got to find a way to communicate back with them. Cass, do you think you can try to use this camera again the way you did before?"

"I can try."

Shelby shrugged in reply. "It's worth a try."

Abby had come to the corner with them.

Cass smiled down at her. "Don't worry, this might mean we've got some help after all. Let's boost me up again so I can see what's going on."

Abby shifted herself until she was in the corner beneath the camera. She braced her arms up against the walls on either side then stared up at Cass with a big grin on her face.

"Step right up."

Cass turned and lifted herself up until she was standing on the younger girl's shoulders again and staring directly into the camera lens.

Following through with what she'd done before, Cass was surprised with how easy it was for her to access the system this time. She surfed along with the circuitry and soon found herself inside the familiar confines of the building's router system.

Having done this once already, Cass quickly found the soft point in the building's firewall again and started to press through until she was outside, into the surrounding network.

Casting about with her awareness, Cass spotted a flickering red light coming through a single node nearby. It ghosted in and out so much, it barely seemed to be there at all. Cass concentrated on it until her awareness came close to it. Suddenly, a voice sounded inside her head.

"*Cassie, is that you?*" Ramona asked.

"*Ramona? What are you doing here? How did you find us?*"

"*Derek got your message. He wasn't sure exactly what to do all by himself, so he reached out to Muller and me.*"

"*We weren't even sure you were alive after we left Pittsburgh. Shelby tried to reach out to you several times but didn't get a response.*"

"*Yeah, things got a little hairy after Pittsburgh. Muller and I both ended up on the run together. We had to do a reset and wipe to create new identities again.*"

"*So you're close by? You can come rescue us?*"

"*We're almost to San Francisco. We should be landing in an hour or so. Where are you?*"

"*Can't you tell where we are from the IP address?*"

"*Derek was able to give us a general vicinity, but wasn't able to zero in any closer than that. Currently, the system nodes around where you are are ancient. It looks like all the buildings in that area are localized to a single address.*"

"*I don't know which building we're in. We were blindfolded with mesh bags over our heads. Our implants were shielded as we came in. I'm not sure exactly which building we're in. We're in some sort of concrete and steel warehouse. The first floor is wide open and then there is a second-floor which is filled with rooms along one long wall.*"

"*Okay, that might help a little bit. I'll see if I can pull up building schematics for that area on my way in. Muller and I should be able to figure out something to localize you when we get there.*"

"*Hopefully they're not all the same,*" Cass said.

"*Hey, positive thinking only from here on out.*"

"*Ramona, you have to hurry.*"

"*We will. We just need to get some people together that Muller knows to help us.*"

"You don't understand. Simon is planning on getting rid of the evidence in the morning. That includes the three of us. He got what he needed from me this afternoon. Now he's going to finish the job he started at the massacre."

"Cassie, if they come, you've got to do something to delay them. We'll get there as soon as we can, but I'm not sure how fast Muller can pull together the kind muscle we're going to need to get past a full Sapiens First security team."

"What about the police?"

"They're not somebody we can trust," Ramona said. *"While I might trust a few of them in the area around Pittsburgh that Muller knows personally, going into a city like San Francisco where we don't know the cops for sure would be problematic. I'm not sure any of them would believe me if I told him what we were looking for. No, we have to do this on our own."*

Cass's system cut off as the connection phased out for a second. When it came back up, Ramona was calling her name.

"Cass, Cass, are you still there?"

"Yeah, I'm still here. I think my system is getting tired or something. This is the second time I've used my ocular implant to break out this way today. It's really taking a toll on me. It must require a great deal of energy to run."

"It's pretty amazing that you can do it at all. I have to talk to Derek about what he did to upgrade your system when he put the original Protocol One file in. Clearly, he made some changes to your firmware that enabled you to do this."

"We'll have to talk to him when we get out of here."

"Deal. All right, we're coming as fast as we can. You keep your head up. If you have to, try to do something to slow things down as much as you can. Just remember, we're coming. Don't give up."

Cass nodded as she felt the link slip away. This time it felt as if she was falling out of control backward down a long shaft.

She landed back in her body, gasping and drenched in sweat. Shelby helped lower her down from Abby's shoulders so that she could sit down.

"Did it work? Was it a message from someone outside?" Abby asked.

Cass nodded. "It was Ramona."

Shelby's eyebrows shot up in surprise. "My cousin's alive?"

Cass nodded. "She and Muller got away. They escaped by switching out their identities again. That's why we couldn't reach out to them. They're on their way here, I think on a jet or something. They're about an hour away from San Francisco then they're going to assemble a team to come get us."

Abby said, "It's almost five in the morning, Cassie. I hope they get here on time."

Shelby reached out and put a hand on Abby's shoulder. "Ramona's reliable and really good at what she does. If anyone can get here on time, she will."

Cass nodded as she tried to pull together what strength she could. Her implants used a lot of energy to run under normal circumstances. None of them had eaten since the previous morning. She didn't have much of a reserve left. She needed food. Hopefully, Ramona wouldn't need her to do too much to help the rescue team when the time came.

Chapter 25

CASS and the others sat in the center of the room, talking until they heard footsteps outside their door. The three women turned to wait as the door opened.

Two figures stood silhouetted in the doorway.

"Come along, ladies. The boss wants to see you."

Cass got up and went over to crouch down next to Abby. "Go ahead and get on my back. I can piggyback you wherever they're going."

Abby slid over on her hands and then reached up to grasp Cass's shoulders. Steadying herself against Shelby, Cass stood with the teenager on her back. She reached back with her arms to grasp the ends of at Abby's thighs, where the metal sockets were attached to her stumps.

The pair of guards backed away from the door and gestured toward the catwalk. They waited for them to exit the room.

Shelby went first, followed by Cass.

One guard led the way while the other moved to follow behind.

They proceeded along the raised walkway and then down the stairs until they reached the first floor.

As they were heading down the stairs, Abby leaned forward and whispered in Cass's ear, "See that forklift? It's got standard contact points on the seat that should match up with my legs. If you can get me over there, I think I can turn it on and run it."

Cass glanced toward the large industrial device, built to lift heavy crates and pallets when the warehouse used to be in operation. It sat in its charging station. That meant it was probably juiced up and ready to go.

"Hey, keep moving." The guard behind them shoved at Abby's back, pushing both of the women forward.

Cass stumbled and nearly fell.

"I'm going as fast as I can," Cass shouted. "She's heavy. I don't want to drop her. "

"Why do I care? Keep moving."

Cass trudged onward after Shelby as they walked across the remaining fifty feet to where Simon and several of his other team members stood watching. Cass paused a step when she saw what Simon held in his hand. It was the pouch with the wand he'd used when they killed Eric and the others at the Saturday Massacre.

She forced herself to keep moving while her mind spun through ways to get them out of here. From the way she saw Shelby's eyes darting around, her girlfriend was thinking similar thoughts. There had to be a way to stop this.

As they came to a stop, Cass glared at Simon. "I thought you said you'd make it painless? You forget that I saw what that machine does. It certainly didn't look painless when I recorded that video."

Simon laughed. "I made you a promise and I will keep that promise. But I am trying to decide if I need more from you that might require me to engage in some persuasion with your companions."

Cass lifted her hands, where they rested under Abby's thighs, to shift the girl's weight on her back a little. She cast a sideways glance back to where the forklift was plugged in on the wall.

Could she make it there before one of the guards caught up to her? All she had to do was get Abby into the seat and delay the guards. The electric engine should start right up.

"Cass, you need to pay attention to me," Simon growled. "If

you don't, I swear all deals are off. There's no way out of here for any of you."

She shifted her eyes back to Simon. "How do I know you'll keep your word this time?"

"You don't. That's not my concern. It will be yours if you don't do exactly as I say."

"What else do you need from me? I told you everything I know and said all the words you told me to say last night."

"While you were sleeping, a reporter from the San Francisco Chronicle started putting out queries searching for you, or at least someone matching your description, with regards to the Saturday Massacre video. Apparently, she believed you held proof the video was real."

Cass smiled. He now had reason to need them alive a little longer.

"Here's the deal I'll make with you, Simon. Let Abby go. She doesn't know anything about this. She's just a kid. No one will believe her if she tells them what little she knows anyway. Let her go. Shelby and I will do whatever you need us to do to verify your side of the story."

Shelby shouted at her, "Cassie, no. Why would you say we'd do such a thing?"

"We don't have a choice, Shel. At least we can save Abby."

Simon scowled at Cass. "You're not really in the position to make any kind of demands of me, girl."

"You already have what you thought you needed with the video. However, with the reporter sniffing around, if you release it now, she's going to poke around and might find out what you did."

Simon started to say something, then closed his mouth. He paused a few seconds before answering. "So, you're telling me you will sit down with this reporter, with me beside you, and tell her everything we agreed to last night?"

Cass nodded. "I'll tell her that and more if you want me to. My only demand is Abby goes free."

Cass's real plan was to delay their execution as long as possible. It appeared that plan, coupled with Simmons concerns about the reporter, might succeed in delaying things for now. Ramona and Muller had to be close to finding them. Ramona had said all she needed was a little time.

The door at the far end of the warehouse opened and one of Simon's men jogged over to whisper something in his ear. Cass dialed up the sensitivity of her auditory implant. She heard the entire conversation.

"Boss, there's something funny going on outside. There's a lot more people around this area than there should be this time of day. These are supposed to be abandoned warehouses."

"What are they doing?"

"Several vehicles have been driving around, circling the buildings. It's as if they're looking for something."

"Who are they? Is it police, Feds?" Simon asked.

The guard shook his head. "Can't tell. The windows are tinted. They don't look like official vehicles, though. I don't think they're cops or anything like that. What do you want us to do about them?"

Simon shook his head. "Don't do anything. Just keep an eye on them. They might be here looking for something else, or they might be here looking for our captives. Either way, we don't want to do anything to confirm where we are. If they knew which building we were in, they'd have come straight here."

An idea formed in Cass's mind, but she needed to act fast. She only had a second or two before Simon returned his attention back to her. She whispered over her shoulder, "Get ready, Abby."

Cass spun around, holding tight to Abby's legs. She sprinted as fast as she could for the corner by the stairs where the forklift sat charging.

The guards shouted behind them, voices echoing through the cavernous warehouse. She'd caught them by surprise and had evaded the pair of guards closest to her.

Checking their pursuit, Cass laughed as she saw Shelby dive in front of the nearest guard, tripping the man up so he fell to the floor.

Turning back, she focused on where she was going. Her heart beat so hard Cass could hear it thumping in her ears.

She ran the last ten feet to the forklift and turned around so Abby could climb off her back.

"Break through those double doors over there, Abby, and head out into the street. I think Ramona and the others are here looking for us, so flag down the first vehicle you see. Got it?"

Abby nodded. "Got it."

Cass turned around as the first guard reached her. He swung at her head with his fist.

She managed to duck under the initial blow and drove forward, shoving her shoulder into his gut, knocking him backward into the stairs.

The two of them landed hard with the guard underneath Cass. She heard the air rush out of his lungs from the impact.

Two other guards had started to approach the forklift, but they were too late.

Cass shouted a cheer as she heard the electric motor whine to life.

Abby had managed to turn it on just like she'd said. Before the guards could reach her, the forklift rolled across the floor, making the two of them dive out of her way. She raced for the far end of the warehouse where two large double doors hung closed and locked. Cass hoped the heavy-duty vehicle could break through.

The deafening sound of gunshots rocked Cass's ears as the remaining guards pulled their pistols out and started firing at the escaping girl.

Abby ducked down in her seat. She crouched as far as she could, but was limited by having to keep her legs engaged with the seat's control surfaces or it would stop.

The bullets flying by didn't seem to faze the teenager, though. Her laughing cheer echoed through the warehouse as the forklift raced away.

Cass got up from where the was tangled with the guard on the floor and raced at another one nearby. He leveled his gun at Abby and the forklift.

He never saw her coming.

Cass dove onto his back and hung on, swinging her arm at his pistol hand, trying to knock off his aim.

He spun around, trying to shake her loose.

Across the warehouse, Abby hit the doors at full speed. The heavy-duty lift popped them open in a crash of splintered wood and metal. Morning sunlight flooded in as the forklift disappeared out the door into the street.

Hands grabbed Cass from behind, hauling her off the guard's back.

Simon's shouts echoed in the warehouse, "Get after that girl. And tie these other two up so they don't cause any more trouble."

Shelby lay on the floor with two guards holding her down.

They pinned Cass's arms behind her, as a pair of guards dragged her over and threw her to the floor beside Shelby.

"Good on you, Cass," Shelby said with a smile.

"At least we got Abby free."

"Silence, you two," Simon shouted. "You may think you've pulled off some sort of an escape, but that girl won't get far. The forklift isn't faster than one of my SUVs. They'll stop her soon enough."

As he said the words, shouts and gunfire sounded outside. Two of his men burst in through a side door nearby. As they entered, the second one spun around and fell to the floor, clutching at his shoulder. Bullets ricochet through the opening as the other guard kept running away from whoever was chasing him.

Several figures appeared in the doorway and crouched just inside. The injured guard on the floor got up and started to run again.

The newcomers gunned him down from behind. More figures appeared in the doorway and turned their gunfire in the direction of the rest of Simon's group.

Cass and Shelby were already on the floor, which was lucky. The guards around them began to return fire at the people in the doorway.

More gunfire drifted in from around where Abby had escaped.

Simon shouted as he backed away from where Shelby and Cass lay on the floor. "Get back to the SUVs."

One of the guards pointed down at Cass and Shelby. "What about them?"

"Shoot them and then get out of here."

The guard turned and leveled this pistol at Cass's head.

She looked up, sure she was dead, as his finger tightened on the trigger.

His body jerked. Several bullets impacted his upper body, until he arched back and fell over onto the concrete floor.

Cass lay there, her eyes meeting his, now sightless in death.

Shouts drew her attention away.

Ramona, Muller, and a dozen armed individuals poured in the side door, racing across the warehouse to chase after Simon and his few remaining guards, as they ran for their vehicles parked just inside building's far side.

Muller and the others sped past, chasing after the retreating Sapiens First team.

Ramona stopped alongside Cass and Shelby. "Are you two all right?"

Shelby smiled. "We are now, cousin. Nothing like arriving in the nick of time."

"Yeah, well, we couldn't figure out which building it was, until that forklift came flying out through the doors. Who is that kid anyway?"

Cass smiled. "She's a friend we found along the way."

"Well, whatever you did to get her loose, it was a good thing. We were about to give up searching here and try to find you some other way."

Cass helped Shelby sit up. Her left arm still dangled uselessly by her side. "Where is Abby, anyway?"

"We have her outside in one of our vehicles. She wanted to turn that forklift around and race back in here after us. I had to leave two people behind just a wrestle her out of it. They put her in the back of one of our vans."

Cass laughed. If there was one thing about Abby she liked the most, it was her willingness to fight and stand up for herself.

New voices came from outside the nearest warehouse door. A woman Cass didn't know walked in, followed by several people with video cameras and lights shining around the broad open space.

The woman pointed to where Cass and Shelby sat on the floor. "They're over here. Come over and set up a shot, John. Larry, you keep that camera on me the whole time. We don't want to miss any of this."

The woman and the two cameramen rushed over. She knelt down next to where Cass and Shelby sat on the floor. "Are you Cass Armstrong?"

Cass nodded.

"And you must be Shelby Moore. Am I right?"

Shelby smiled. "That's me."

"I'm Meredith Langston and I'm here to get your story for the whole world to hear. When you didn't show up to meet with me yesterday, I had a feeling there was a great story behind it. The people want to know exactly what happened to you here. Are you ready to share your story with the world?"

Cass glanced at Shelby.

Shelby reached out and gave Cass's hand a squeeze. She nodded.

Cass turned to the reporter and smiled. "Where do you want me to start?"

Chapter 26

CASS SIPPED her coffee as she stared out the apartment window. A message pinged her implant's system.

She smiled. It was from Abby and contained an attachment. Cass brought it up in her implant to view.

Abby stood on her brand new cybernetic legs, next to her father. He sat in a wheelchair, in front of their home, back in Indiana. Matilda, the diner waitress they'd met, stood behind Mr. Cleary's wheelchair with her hand on his shoulder.

Cass, Shelby, and most of all, Abby, had been surprised to discover Mr. Cleary was still alive. The announcement of his death in the news had been part of a plan by Federal investigators to keep him in protective custody during his recovery from the injuries sustained when the Sapiens First team attacked the farm.

The message from Abby read:

Just wanted to tell you Dad was out of the hospital. He'll be in the wheelchair for a couple of weeks, but the docs say he should be back on his feet before we know it.

Neighbors are helping us with the crops in the meantime. Everyone loves my new legs. You won't believe how crazy fast I can run.

Hope you and Shelby can come to visit soon. Dad wants to thank you in person with a home-cooked meal here at the house.

Let me know when you can make the trip.

Abby

Cass chuckled as she read it.

Shelby walked into the kitchen with a big grin on her face. "I just got the cutest message from Abby."

"I got it, too. I'm glad her dad is finally home from the hospital. They look so happy to be back together. Plus, it looks like that diner lady, Matilda, finally got him to slow down enough for her to catch up to him."

It had been two weeks since Cass had left him sitting in a pool of blood inside the front door of his house. So much had changed for all of them since then. Cass marveled at how quickly their lives had returned to a sort of routine once they'd been able to stop running.

"Don't forget, Cassie, we have that TV thing this afternoon. Meredith got us on that national talk show to talk about cyber human rights."

"I remember. It's hard to keep it all straight, though, Shel. How many interviews have we done since Meredith released her exposé?"

"I've lost count. You've done more than me, which I'm thrilled with."

"You would be. You know I hate being the center of attention."

Shelby laughed. "You'll survive. Besides, this is what we wanted. Everything is working out, and the bad guys are finally going away for what they did to Eric and my parents."

Cass shook her head. So much had happened so fast after their rescue and their story hit the various news channels online.

Federal authorities hunted down the people involved with Simon Cantwell, tracking his network, thanks to the files Cass had secretly downloaded from his computer during her interrogation in the warehouse.

Cass worried some that they hadn't been able to track him down yet. Apparently, the name Simon Cantwell was an alias. No one knew who he really was. It was like he'd disappeared completely.

Shelby came over and wrapped her arms around Cass from behind, pulling her close. "Come on, let's get dressed and ready to go. They're sending a car over to take us to the studio."

"I'll be ready. I hope they don't ask me too much about my family, though."

"You know they're going to. The Feds arrested your dad two days ago. He's charged with conspiring with Simon to conceal evidence about the Saturday Massacre. According to what I saw, he was involved in other things, too, now that they've got the organization's records."

"Yeah, but Sterling Noble skated away free and clear, so far. I can't believe he's gotten away with pretending this was just a rogue element within an otherwise peaceful organization."

Shelby sighed. Cass knew she wanted him charged for her parents' death, along with the secret Sapiens First group within the Boston Police Department who'd done the deed.

"Cass, you know how bad I want him to get caught in this, too. There's a lot more investigation to go. There's still a chance they'll find something to tie him to all of this."

Cass nodded. So much of this brought up conflicting emotions for her, especially when her father had been arrested and taken to jail.

Then there was her mother and Elena. They had mostly been left alone by the investigators, aside from being questioned about what they knew. They'd been kicked out of their home in the enclave by the local Sapiens Movement Council. Her mother and sister had moved into an apartment in the nearby town outside of Philadelphia.

Cass's mother had reached out to her on two occasions. Cass wanted to talk to her, to thank her again for helping her get away from Simon, but it didn't feel right to do it over a face chat or phone call. There was still the way she'd treated Cass in the beginning, when she'd first discovered her daughter's cybernetic enhancements.

Shelby turned Cass around so she faced her direction. "What's got you so sad, hon?"

"It's my mom. She sent me a message again. There was also one from Elena. The problem is, I don't want to talk with them right now. Especially not with Elena. Does that make me a horrible person?"

"No, not horrible. You will have to eventually, though."

Cass nodded. Elena was the hardest part of it all. That kind of betrayal was hard to take. No matter what her sister said to her, Cass knew it would be years before they'd come back to the relationship they once had, if at all.

"Hey, buck up," Shelby said. "No more sad thoughts. Let's go out to dinner after the interview today. We'll be down near the waterfront. You like seafood and we can sit where we can watch the sunset over the water."

Shelby reached out with her cybernetic hand to grip Cass's hand. "Everything's going to be all right. You know that, right?"

Cass nodded. So much had changed for them. Many of the talk show interviews came with an appearance fee. That income, plus the Federal reward money they were due to receive for uncovering a terrorist organization, had been a pleasant surprise. She and Shelby would be able to go back to school now if they wanted to.

She wasn't worried about herself anymore. She worried more about the reaction to her interviews she'd seen online. The members of the Sapiens Movement had mostly dug in even deeper behind their views on cyber humans. Their press releases tried to twist her words into some sort of a betrayal. They said she was evidence of what happens to someone when they get an implant.

Cass had quickly realized, while reading through some of the comments and articles from the other side, that she would never be finished fighting against prejudice and hatred. The only thing she could do was keep standing up for the people she cared about the most, and that started right here, with Shelby.

Cass pulled Shelby close. "The only thing I need in this whole world is you, Shel. We don't have to run anymore. We can get on with our lives in a place where people accept us for who we are."

"That's all that matters to me, too."

Cass rested her head against Shelby's shoulder and looked out the window at the city, full of people of all kinds, with a vibrant community of cyber humans they'd found within San Francisco. On the streets outside, people with all sorts of cyber enhancements went about their days, safe and secure in a community that accepted them without reservation.

She marveled at how far she'd come in less than a year. It had been a long, scary trip, but in the end, Cass Armstrong had gained more than she'd lost. Together, she and Shelby could take on the world.

The End?

It doesn't have to be.
Read on for an author's note on the writing of this series.
And visit JamieDavisBooks.com to find many more books you'll like.

Afterword

A Note From The Author

This project, the Sapiens Run trilogy, started as a project inspired by my daughter's call for me to write a book or series with LGBTQ+ characters. Okay, I can do that. I mean, how hard could it be for a middle-aged, white heterosexual guy to pull off?

I'll wait while your laughter dies down.

I took the challenge seriously and enlisted my daughter and her fiancé to read over the chapters as I wrote them to make sure the relationship between Cass and Shelby rang true to them. I wrote it from my own view on a healthy relationship full of love, trust, and mutual support. I wondered how that would translate. I wanted to be authentic.

Aside from a few notes on some additional details, most of the relationship I'd created between Cass and Shelby rang true to them.

Why?

Because love is love.

There's no straight love, or gay love, or cyber love. There's just glorious, wonderful human love, perhaps God's greatest gift to us.

Being human ties us all together with similar needs for closeness and loving relationships. It doesn't matter if you're straight, gay, trans, questioning, or cybernetically enhanced. The basis of humanity, what makes us all the same, is our ability to love another.

So, what did I learn while writing this series?

It's simple.

The old cliche says "love conquers all." It certainly conquered this old guy's deep, unconscious preconceptions.

Thank you, Saralynn and Hannah, for reminding me to be open to exploring loving relationships within my characters. You've helped me remember to build worlds rich with love, present in all its glorious variations.

Also by Jamie Davis

Sapiens Run Trilogy

Book 1 - *Cyber's Change*

Book 2 - *Cyber's Escape*

Book 3 - *Cyber's Underground*

—

The Delivery Mage (5 Urban Fantasy books)

Book 1 - *Deliver or Die*

—

The Broken Throne Series (5 Urban Fantasy books)

Read book 1 - *The Charm Runner*

—

The Accidental Traveler LitRPG Trilogy

(with C.J. Davis)

Read book 1 - *The Accidental Thief*

—

Accidental Champion LitRPG Trilogy 2

(with C.J. Davis)

Read book 1 - *Accidental Duelist*

—

Extreme Medical Services Series (8 Urban Fantasy books)

Read book 1 - Extreme Medical Services

—

Eldara Sister Series (2 Historical Fantasy books)

Read book 1 - *The Nightingale's Angel*

—

Follow on Facebook for updates, news, and upcoming book excerpts

Facebook.com/jamiedavisbooks

—

Leave a Review

I Need Your Help ...

Without reviews indie books like this one are almost impossible to market.

Leaving a review will only take a minute — it doesn't have to be long or involved, just a sentence or two that tells people what you liked about the book, to help other readers know why they might like it, too. It also helps us write more of what you love.

The truth is, VERY few readers leave reviews. Please help us out by being the exception.

Thank you in advance!

Jamie Davis

About the Author

Jamie Davis is a nurse, retired paramedic, author, and nationally recognized medical educator who began teaching new emergency responders as a training officer for his local EMS program. He loves everything fantasy and sci-fi and especially the places where stories intersect with his love of medicine or gaming.

Jamie lives in a home in the woods in Maryland with his wife, three children, and dog.

He loves hearing from readers and going to cons and events where he meets up with fans. Reach out and say "hi." Visit Jamie-DavisBooks.com for more books, free offers and more!

Follow Jamie Online
www.jamiedavisbooks.com

facebook.com/jamiedavisbooks

twitter.com/podmedic

instagram.com/podmedic